HeartsBlood
BOOK TWO

Remortality

**Previously published as Blood Red Strawberry
by Lena Fox**

Published by Fairies and Fantasy Pty Ltd 2021
ISBN: 978-1-922390-30-1 (paperback)
ISBN: 978-1-922390-31-8 (hardcover)
Remortality (Heartsblood Book 2) copyright © 2018 Selina Fenech.
All rights reserved. www.selinafenech.com
Formatting design © 2021 www.kiladesigns.com.au

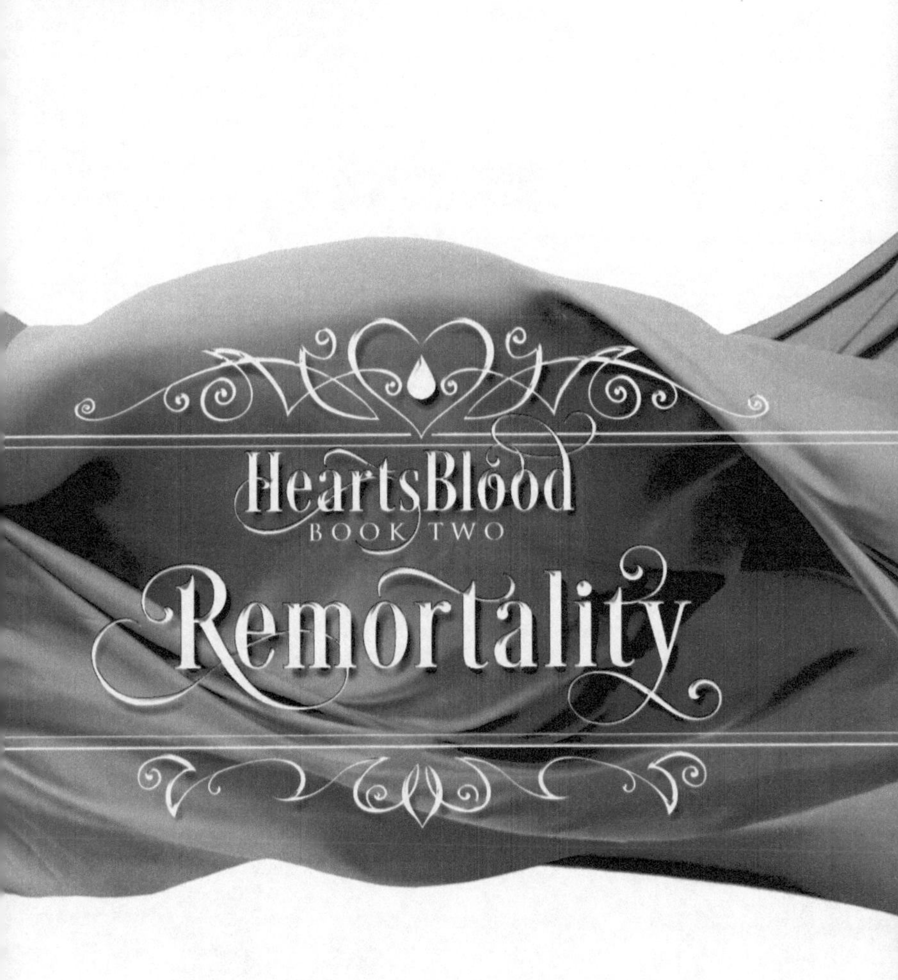

SELINA A. FENECH WRITING AS

LENA FOX

1

KAITLYN

"Death won't part us. You hear me? Fight this. Fight for me!" I cried, tears streaming down my cheeks.

Kneeling before me, a man with the face of a Greek god looked up with hooded eyes, his blond ringlets shiny and wet from the light rain that fell. The love and desperation in his expression was as clear as the blood spread across the chest of his civil war officer's uniform.

I cupped his face in my hands, feeling his rough stubble.

His head swayed weakly. "You are everything I wanted. To be with you. To be yours. And you mine. I have fought, and I have lost. I fear you will lose me now ..."

"No. I can't lose you. We belong together." I leaned down and planted a soft kiss on his lips, tasting his tears. "Wherever you go, I go too."

I slipped the knife easily from his belt and plunged it just as easily into my heart.

I fell into his arms.

"Cut! I think we've got everything we need." The scene finished. Applause broke out. I blinked rapidly, so lost in the part that for a second, I couldn't remember where or even who I was. Cameras and lights surrounded me in a warehouse-sized studio.

Getting to my feet, I handed the prop knife back to Miles, the leading man, to reset the scene. We held our places, waiting to hear from the director whether we were going to do another take. Make-up came to spritz us with water again to simulate being wet from the rain that would be added in post-production. This was the last day of filming, doing pick-ups and capturing some final takes for the big moments. This scene was the most important. It had to be perfect, moving, painful.

I had plenty of painful memories to draw upon.

How things had changed. My nerves tingled, and a wide smile spread on my face. No matter how many times I told myself this was real, it still felt like a crazy dream. I was an actress, and rapidly becoming a successful one.

There'd been a time when I'd been sure it would

never happen. Not just because my agent back then had been a slimy weasel unable to get me good roles. But because that same slimy weasel had sent me on a job that had nearly ended my life. It was supposed to be an evening with make-believe vampires. Only—surprise!—there'd been a *real* vampire there, and he had imprisoned me in his house of horrors, feasting on my blood again and again.

I'd been sure I was going to die, that I would never escape the torment of having my blood taken against my will. Of being chained and deprived of my freedom. Of being some *thing's* food. Or the fear that eventually, he would stop just sipping at my veins and open them up to drain me dry.

He only hadn't because my blood had changed him. It made him more human. It made him feel things he hadn't felt for centuries. And then my blood had somehow cured his vampirism completely.

Owen was human now, and he was the man I loved. And who I'd been missing like crazy.

I'd been kept apart from Owen by this fantastic role my new agent had gotten me. He was an amazing agent, but really, anyone would have been a step up from the last guy. An agent willing to send you to your death is not the person you want representing you. That's Hollywood 101.

Spencer, the director, was busy going over the dailies with the director of photography, checking over the last footage, confirming they had everything.

"That's a wrap!" he called.

People whooped around the set which still buzzed with activity. The night wasn't over for most here, not yet. The few extras on set cleared out, but all around, the crew were busy with their tasks, and I marveled at the human machine we had become, all the pieces ticking away together to create a work of art. A story in motion.

But for me, my job was done.

Stepping off the set, I grabbed my dressing gown from the back of my chair. I stifled a yawn. This shoot had run late and been taxing physically and emotionally.

Miles joined me, grabbing a bottle off his chair and taking a long swig of water.

"It was such a pleasure working with you." He extended his hand, grinning warmly. I took it, but after a brief shake I pulled him in for a firm hug. He had been awesome. I had been awesome. I was so excited for this film.

"See you at the premiere." I shook his hand again and headed off.

"Principal actors leaving set," the assistant director called.

Movement around the room did stop then, briefly, as everyone paused to applaud. I blushed, and smiled at the throngs of people who made me feel as though

I truly belonged there, on that set and on that film. That I'd earned my place here and I did it well.

I opened the studio door to rejoin reality outside. I knew it was late, but the darkness of night still surprised me. On set it had felt like it had just been daytime.

Spencer caught up to me on my way out. He beamed. "Excellent job, Kaitlyn. Excellent. I love your work. Love it."

Kaitlyn. The name change had been Owen's idea, and it had been a good one. I used to be known as Kitty, and looking back, I could see now why I got so many casting offers for low-budget slasher flicks and porn.

I said, "I love your work too. Although, I know that's obvious, and I've said it about a million times, every time we talk."

He chuckled.

"I'm so grateful you decided to cast me as your lead. It means everything to me." And it would mean everything to my career. Spencer's like or dislike of an actor had big repercussions in Hollywood. If he told other directors I was good, they'd ask to have me sent a script for their projects. But I didn't have anything lined up off the back of this shoot yet, which made me anxious. The old struggling actress inside me wanted to take any offer that came my way, but my agent had assured me it was best to wait, that some amazing roles would be coming …

if I impressed Spencer.

The way he beamed at me like a proud father, I felt confident I had.

"I don't know where you were hidden away before this" he said, and I choked back a small laugh. "But don't go hiding again. You're made to act."

He hugged me, then I turned away and headed for my trailer. I was dying to get out of this rigid, scratchy, but admittedly gorgeous, period gown.

When I opened the door, I had another reason to get out of this dress.

"Owen!"

He stood in the middle of the trailer, wearing a casual gray suit, and twirling a single rose cheekily in one hand.

I hadn't seen him for three weeks. Three long weeks, while I filmed on location in Virginia. Coming with me would have meant he had to hide out in my trailer all day, every day. Despite being human now, he was still avoiding the sun, and any kind of publicity. He worried about the news of his return to humanity getting back to the wrong people. He was still playing the part of a vampire, and sometimes I also wondered if he avoided the sun in case the cure wasn't permanent.

Even with how far we'd come, we were still a few blocks away from Easy Street, but I didn't care. The sight of his beautiful face and smitten eyes left me breathless.

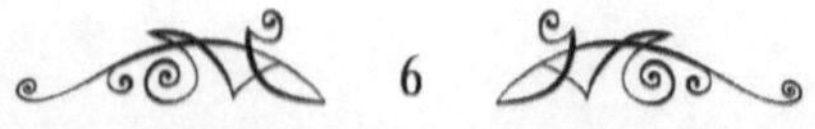

Remortality

I rushed into his arms. He bent to kiss me then paused, a frown appearing. His thumb wiped across my cheek and came away red.

My heart flopped. "Oh no, it's prop blood. Fake. Not even *my* fake blood. Someone else's fake blood. Everything is okay."

Blood was a bit of a trigger for him, given our pasts.

He nodded as though he understood, but the frown remained.

The moment had cooled, and while I longed to press my lips against his and have him rip this bodice from me, I satisfied myself with a soft, slow kiss on his cheek.

He breathed in deep as I did. "You're not wearing the perfume I gave you?"

"Must have forgotten." I shrugged. It was a beautiful, unique scent, and I normally wore it every day because it reminded me of Owen when we were apart, but I'd been so focused on the shoot. "What are you doing here? I didn't think I'd see you until I got back to the ranch next week."

He ran a finger down the side of my face and looked at me with those cornflower blue eyes. "I've arranged a special gift for you."

"Oh?"

He smirked, devilishly. "A secret surprise."

I regarded him. Owen loved to give me presents. He often cooked for me, and since he had been

unable to eat regular food for centuries, he had now become almost as much of a foodie as I was. *Almost.* But his resources never ceased to surprise me, nor his creativity. He'd taken to being human again with a thirst for new and beautiful things as unquenchable as his thirst for blood had once been. And he loved to share that with me.

I purred, "You'll tell me now though, right? Don't keep me in suspense."

He just laughed and took my hand. "Come on, we have to go."

"Fine, be secretive then. But I have to change, real quick. This dress belongs to the set. My reputation can't afford being labeled a wardrobe thief. Also, it's itchy as hell."

Owen shrugged, a small smile on his face. "I don't mind watching."

I didn't mind him watching me change either. Once upon a time, he had kept me without access to much clothing, and I'd hated him for that, but he was a different man then. Not even a man—a monster. Now, as I undressed before him, deliberately taking my time to undo each button before allowing the bodice to fall away to the floor, I loved that he let his eyes wander up and down my body, and didn't hide the desire he had for me.

He wanted *me*, and not my blood, and there was a huge difference.

The early spring weather was crisp and cool in the evenings, but I felt bright and happy so chose a light sundress, regardless of the sun having been down for hours. I didn't bother with a bra, just slipped the dress over my body with a flirty wiggle.

Owen stalked up to me, desire heavy in his eyes.

I leaned into him. He had body heat now, and I couldn't help but remember how cold his skin had been when we'd first met. Cold as the grave. I smiled as I soaked up the warmth of his humanity.

My head tilted back so I could look up at his face, and his lips claimed mine in a dizzying kiss. He tasted like red wine, and I drank him in. My breasts flattened against his broad chest, and my hands rested along the strong curves of his shoulders. The reassuring thump of his heartbeat against my flesh grounded me, even as his kiss swept me away.

My eyes fluttered closed. When I opened them again, I saw us in the mirror, kissing. I stared at the sight, mesmerized. I never did see vampire-Owen in front of a mirror, to discover if the old myth was true, but every time I saw him in one now, it came home to me all over again that he was human. That we had a life together.

I parted from his kiss but didn't leave his arms. "So, now what?"

Owen grinned. "I hope you're ready for an adventure."

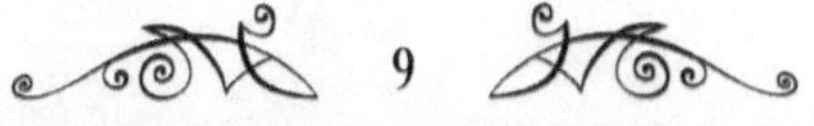

2

OWEN

The door of the trailer banged shut behind us. Kaitlyn giggled as I led her along by her hand toward a shiny black limo. She skipped, light on her feet, but her body swayed and her eyes stayed closed a moment too long each time she blinked. It was late, and she'd been working hard. I should have waited until the morning, but no. I couldn't have. I couldn't wait a moment longer to see her again.

I opened the door for her, and she scooted across the back seat to let me in beside her. She kicked her shoes off and dug her toes into the soft carpeting, smiling blissfully.

I put my arm around her shoulders and tapped on the closed partition. The driver got us moving, and Kaitlyn sank into me. The adrenaline from being on set, which I could tell had kept her going until now, must have worn out. The heat and weight of her head on my chest felt so right and perfect, so real. We sat silent together, content in each other's company.

It was late at night, more morning really, and barely anything could be seen through the nearly-black tinted windows. I hadn't requested a car with such dark tinting like I would have once done, but I'd received one anyway. It was like a relic from my sunless past. One I wished I could shed, like so much I had left behind since then, but one that still provided a privacy and anonymity that was convenient.

The driver took a hard turn and the small regional airport came into view. Kaitlyn raised her eyebrows at me. "Just how far away is this surprise? Because I only have my purse."

"Don't worry. Everything is sorted." I gave her my smuggest grin, then pulled her in closer, feeling a sudden surge of protectiveness for her.

I'd missed her while she was on location for this new film. Honestly, I'd wished she wouldn't go. That she wouldn't leave my side. But I could never again control her freedom as I'd done before. Ever since I'd been cured, I've had to keep a low profile. I couldn't let the other vampires know I was human any more than I could let humans know I had once been a vampire. I was existing outside both worlds.

Remortality

I had to avoid her places of work, or even being seen with her in public, lest a photo of us together was taken and shared in this new world of social media, online content, and facial-recognition software. I found the new technologies of the internet and intelligent software useful for business, but social media held little interest to me. I liked my privacy, now more than ever.

And I worried about Kaitlyn's career. The more famous she got, the harder it would be to hide our relationship. To keep me, and her special blood hidden. So far, she had been mostly off the paparazzi's radar, just another up-and-coming starlet. But with Spencer's film, things were already changing. Yet, I could never say a word that would come between Kaitlyn and her dreams.

She probably knew the risks as well. At least in part. But I wasn't helping by holding back so much information from her either. So much about the world of night I had left behind. Of how I had to dismantle the life and businesses I'd developed over centuries and make Owen Raine disappear. Of how much danger Kaitlyn might still be in, just for the scent of her sweet blood. I wished she'd wear the Nemexia perfume more often, but I didn't want to explain to her why.

We were waved through the gates and the driver took us right onto the runway, up to the small

jet I had chartered. I used to have my own plane, complete with blackout windows safe for flying even during daylight hours. But like so many of my possessions from that time, it was gone. Most of my assets had been liquidated, and the wealth that remained was hidden under various new names and corporate entities. Sacrifices had to be made. I didn't mind. Despite some remaining limitations and fears, life felt fresh and new, and I had Kaitlyn by my side. That was enough.

I did miss the strength and speed that I'd had as a vampire, but this body was still strong. I got out of the car, and when Kaitlyn followed me, I scooped her up into my arms. She giggled delightfully, and I carried her up the steps into the jet.

"I've never been in a private plane before," she said. I put her back on her feet. She seemed more awake now, alert and excited as she explored the interior, then flopped down with a happy sigh into a wide, cream leather seat. "This is lush."

The only details I paid much attention to were the crystal-clear windows. Sunrise would come while we were in the air. A chill ran through my bones. Part of me still worried that one day, while I stood under the warmth of the sun, the cure would wear off and I would burn to ashes.

I buried that fear and sat down beside my love. "You've seen nothing yet."

Remortality

The captain's voice came over the speaker to announce our departure, so we buckled up as the jet began to taxi around and build speed. Kaitlyn sat back in her chair, closed her eyes, and squeezed my hand as we lifted off the ground and zoomed for the sky. Once the sensation of acceleration slowed and the seat belt light went off, she sighed and stretched.

She propped herself up on her elbow on the armrest between us, her nose brushing softly against mine. "Just how private is this plane?"

She took my hand, bringing it up onto her breast as she brushed her lips over mine. I groaned into her mouth. I had missed her body as much as I'd missed the rest of her.

Our mouths met fully, desire pressing us into each other, an undeniable force. Kaitlyn pushed the armrest up and threw her leg over mine. Her silky sundress slipped right up to her hips, her thighs bared, smooth and milky. I grabbed at her, pulling her off her chair and into my lap, moaning as she pressed against me. I tangled my fingers in her dark hair, placing kisses down her neck and across her cleavage. As a vampire, I'd sunk my teeth into her there, and the temptation to do so again came over me like a wave, but for an all-different form of desire. Her breath was a gasp as my hands ran up between her thighs.

The rustle of the velvet partition curtain opening

broke us apart just as the flight attendant appeared, pulling a trolley through after her.

Kaitlyn sighed dramatically as she moved back into her seat and re-adjusted her dress, but I knew she wouldn't be upset for long. The trolley arrived beside us. On it, champagne cooled in a silver bucket filled with heart-shaped ice, with two very fine-stemmed glasses set to one side. Chocolate-covered strawberries were piled high on a wooden board between a range of cheeses, small triangles of crisp bread, Russian caviar, and cured meats sliced so thin they were nearly transparent.

"I may not be familiar with private planes, but now we're in territory I know all about," Kaitlyn said, eyeing the food with a lust akin to how she'd just looked at me.

"Excuse the interruption." The attendant smiled pleasantly, a glint in her eye showing she knew full well what she'd just put a halt to. "If there is anything else you need, just press the call button. I hope you both have a wonderful flight."

She had a sweet face and blond hair in a perfectly trimmed pixie cut. Well dressed, well mannered, well kept. An opposing image of my thrall, Loretta, in her grimy rags, came to me. As a vampire, I'd still had feelings, of a sort. Anger, desire, even sadness to some extent. The one aspect of humanity that vampires truly lacked was empathy. With my empathy returned now, so too came the guilt for keeping Loretta as I had done. She was the only thrall I had kept. For the most part, how I had employed people was very normal in the running of my businesses. Normal humans working normal jobs for a reclusive CEO they never met, or only saw at night. I only used my enthralling powers on people who discovered too much and needed the memory of those discoveries removed. Like those I'd fed on.

But Loretta was different. She had begun as one of my normal employees, until I discovered the depth of her violence and psychosis. I'd kept her as a slave more to keep her from other humans than because I needed her. Even still, the misery of her slavery, and how it had ended, still haunted me thanks to my new-found empathy.

So did the knowledge that other vampires often kept a whole stable of enthralled humans for far more unsavory uses.

Kaitlyn waved a massive strawberry under my nose. The intoxicating scent drew me from my thoughts, and made my whole body tingle and my mouth water.

I ran a finger down her cheek and said, "There is no strawberry sweeter than you."

She made the cutest cooing sound before the glint of mischief returned to her beautiful green eyes. "And there's no cheese cheesier than you."

I opened my mouth to quip back, but she silenced me by sliding the strawberry between my lips. I bit down. Tart and tangy juice filled my mouth. Dark chocolate coated my tongue with its bitter decadence. The flavors met and melded and I let them rest on my tongue. As a vampire, food had turned to ash in my mouth. Strawberries had been my favorite food before I'd been turned, and they still were. But the small, wild strawberries available back then could not compare to the massive, succulent fruit available now. Being able to taste such beauty would alone have been worth becoming human again for.

The sticky insides of the soft cheese Kaitlyn had just placed in her mouth coated her fingers, and she licked them sensually. Her expression of indulgent happiness made me smile as well. She rested her head back, closed her eyes, and then did not open them again.

Her breathing slowed and I realized she'd fallen asleep. Her head slipped a little to the side, exposing her long neck, and the scars there of my first savage feeding on her. They were covered by make-up from the set, but I could see the raised lines and marks beneath. Scars that would never fade.

I called the attendant for a pillow, and tucked it between her head and my shoulder.

I watched the darkness outside the window for a long time, until the sky slowly brightened. Soon, the rising sun's strong rays turned everything pink and gold, the sky pale and serene, patterned with puffs and ribbons of cloud, tinted peach.

At that moment, my heart was so full I honestly thought that nothing could ever mar the perfection of my new life.

I should have known better.

3

KAITLYN

The bump of the wheels hitting the runway woke me from my sleep. It had been the deep sleep of total mind and body exhaustion—the result of completing the grueling shoot. I peered groggily out the window as the roar of the jets firing up in reverse slowed us down.

Sunset.

I turned to Owen. "Where on Earth are we that it's sunset already?"

He chuckled. "You slept through the whole day. Which really is the best way to fly if you can. Although, I don't know who is more vampire right now, with these hours you keep."

"You still didn't answer my question. Where are we? Where are we going?" I didn't want to nag, but

the mystery was becoming a bit too much when I'd been flown to who knew where for a whole day. Obviously, I knew we were flying *somewhere,* but I'd thought it was maybe back home, or at least in the same country. I still felt half asleep, and disoriented, and being taken somewhere so distant without my knowledge was starting to rub me the wrong way.

Owen became serious. "We're in Slovakia. It's not much farther to your present now. Please trust me, Strawberry."

Slovakia? I looked out the window again as the last golden edge of sun slipped away behind craggy mountains.

"Okay already. Let's get this adventure started then."

I still didn't have a clue where we were going next, or what the present he was determined to surprise me with was, but I would try to be patient. Knowing Owen, it would be worth it.

The plane came to a stop and we got off into a crisply cold evening, filled with shadows and the scent of wood fires. The airport was small—one runway, a few hangars, our plane, and only one smaller jet were in view. An older-style town car trundled toward us.

"You could've given me a little clue about our destination when I put this skimpy dress on," I said, shivering.

Owen didn't reply. His head was turned to one

side, and when I glanced over at his face, caught his eyes scanning the distance, and his lips had compressed flat. His body went rigid with tension and his nostrils quivered. Fear flared along my spine as I tried to see what he was looking at.

A shape separated itself from the deeper shadows beside the other plane. My heart pounded as I watched, a primal, animal fear shivering through me for no apparent reason. It was a man's figure, but he was too far away for me to make out much else.

"Owen? Who is that?"

His body relaxed as the man walked toward the tiny administration office.

Owen turned to me again and did a double-take, as though he'd forgotten I was there. "You're freezing." Without another word, he stripped off his jacket and draped it over my shoulders. I could feel the lingering body warmth he'd left in it and hugged it close to me.

Our luggage was loaded into the car, and I saw that Owen had packed my set of suitcases from home for me. We were driven to what counted as a terminal and passed through what counted for customs with a cursory glance and a few quick stamps in our passports, which Owen had also packed. There was only one man in the tiny building that I could see, and he was a very large man, entirely not the shape of the shadow-man we'd seen outside. The other man could have been a security guard, or a groundsman. There were a million other plausible reasons why he wasn't this man we saw now, but I still felt unsettled.

Before I knew it, we were back in the car. For a while, nothing but darkness flashed by our windows. Then a town came into view, all stone houses and fairy tale cobbled streets, filmed over by a thin fog that crept along the sides of the road as we climbed ever higher along a tall mountain. The lights of civilization dropped away behind us, but the car crept higher and higher yet, the headlights picking up a terrifying drop on my side of the road. My whole body tingled with anticipation, as though I stood on the edge of a great adventure, and the night invited me to leave everything behind.

Tall trees stood thick on the other side of the road, their tops pointing at a sky that held more fine veils of obscuring mist, and a bloated white moon, full and ripe. Stars pricked against the velvety black. The sense that we were leaving the world behind strengthened as we passed an old church. It stood alone, framed by moonlight and glowing with an unearthly, silver pallor. A large cross riding atop it shimmered like a portent.

The car halted before massive wrought-iron gates. They were abutted by a high stone wall on either side, topped with fanciful little curlicues and scrolls of more iron. I heard the driver buzz us in, and the gates swung open with a soft clang. We drove along the driveway, which swept through an alley of trees with long and skeletal limbs, holding only the tight buds of new spring leaves, still unopened. Coming around a tight corner, I nearly dislocated my jaw when it dropped so hard and fast at the view before me.

It's a castle!

I mean, I didn't know the exact definition of what counted as a castle, or palace, or chateau, or whatever, but this thing had god-darn princess towers. And it was bigger than any mansion I'd ever seen. I was calling it a castle.

I gulped. "Um … is that … is this yours?"

"No." Owen leaned across me to look out my side of the car as well. He landed a soft kiss on my cheek then said, "It's yours."

"It's *WHAT?*"

His eyes lit with passion. "It was mine. It was the first thing of great value I bought for myself once I became wealthy. I haven't lived here for centuries, but have visited on and off every decade or so. When I was having my properties sold to remove Owen Raine from this world, sentimentality took over and I couldn't part with this one. So, I came up with this solution. This castle, these lands, and the trust which funds the maintenance of them, are all now in your name."

What did a girl say to that? I had no words. The only thing my mouth knew to do then was kiss Owen in the deepest way I could.

Owen smiled beneath my lips. Between kisses, he said, "You gave me back my life and my heart. Giving you a castle is the least I could do in return."

"Well, when you put it that way …" I mumbled back.

Gravel crunched under the car's wheels as it braked in front of a wide stone staircase which led to two tall wooden doors, carved with blossoming fruit trees. The moment the car stopped, I was out. It was significantly cooler than it had been back in Virginia, and the mist, running low and thick, clung to the grass and flowerbeds. It gathered near the feet of a tall statue of a goddess-like woman, surrounded by shorter statues that looked like something between cherubs and demons.

Owen appeared by my side, and we headed to the entrance. The doors had large, brass knockers, covered with verdigris, except the base of the rings which were polished bright through use. I looked from the door to Owen, wondering if we were supposed to knock. *Did one knock at one's own castle?* My question was answered when the door swung open and a gaunt face appeared atop an equally waiflike body.

The woman was incredibly tall, and incredibly old. Her face was seamed and marked by age, but her eyes were sharp and clear. She wore a finely cut gray dress, covered by a white apron neatly tied at one side of her narrow waist.

"Dobry wieczór, Owen," she said.

Owen tilted his head to me. *"Po angielsku proszę."*

Eyeing me, she nodded. She spoke in a low voice and heavy accent, "Hello, and welcome home. Please to come in. Shall I present for you some foods after your travel?"

I was too busy being surprised about Owen speaking—crap, I felt so ignorant, I didn't even know what language—to answer. I wondered how many languages he may have learned in his centuries-long life. Inadequacy punched me in the gut.

Owen replied, "Thank you, Marianne. We're good. Please, you and your husband can finish up and head home. We will be fine alone for the night." Owen nodded to our driver as he walked past us, taking our luggage in. "Thank you, Tomas."

Somewhat shorter than Marianne, stocky, and just as old, the man smiled at Owen as though bestowing a blessing on him, then bowed himself away.

"He doesn't speak much English," Owen whispered to me.

Marianne curtseyed, sharp and to the point. "You'll find everything in order. Kitchen is stocked as your wishes. I collect my things and go. Good night to you."

She headed off down the hall. When they were

both out of earshot, I said, "Aren't they a bit old to be working here?"

Owen's eyes crinkled at the corners. "Oh? I didn't notice."

"You didn't notice?"

He shook his head, putting an innocent expression on his face that I wasn't buying at all. "They've been working here a long time—long enough to think I'm the son of the previous owner. They practically live here, and still do good work and seem happy to do it, so I haven't thought to replace them."

"Well, they are certainly much nicer than Loretta."

Hurt flashed across his face.

"I'm so sorry," I said, realizing my mistake the second the words were out of my mouth. Now that Owen was human again, the last thing he needed was for me to point out his misdeeds from when he was a vampire.

He shrugged it off. "No, it's okay. I have a lot to make up for in my life. Come on, let's go inside."

I hesitated. The last time I stepped into a place all decked out like a gothic castle I'd ended up as a captive to a vampire. This place didn't just look the part—it was set in a landscape that could have been hijacked from the set of some old horror flick I never wanted to see because, hell, I'd already lived it. But really, what were the chances of that happening again?

Remortality

Owen's hand met the small of my back, and he gently pushed me inside. To my relief, the interior was bright and classy, nary a gothic candelabra to be seen. LED downlights made bright, polished marble surfaces sparkle. An enormous, glittering chandelier hung between a double staircase, that swirled in elegant symmetry up both sides of the foyer. The carved spires and railings ran upward and then formed lovely half-turns that eventually led to the second floor. Amid the decadence, there was a modern elegance to everything that I found comforting.

The banks of windows were draped in burgundy velvet which pooled on the white marble floors. Gold leafing accented the hand-carved wooden furniture, which were either antiques or fantastic reproductions. A subtle brocade wallpaper led the eye upward to the ceiling moldings, filled with frolicking cherubs and winding roses.

"Would you like a tour?"

My stomach grumbled audibly in reply.

Owen laughed. "Let's start at the kitchen then."

We left our shoes in the foyer, and I delighted in feeling the heated floors under my toes.

It wasn't a long walk through the main hall to the final door on the right. The kitchen was contemporary and fresh, so much so that it surprised me. It could have easily appeared in *Modern Chefs Magazine*.

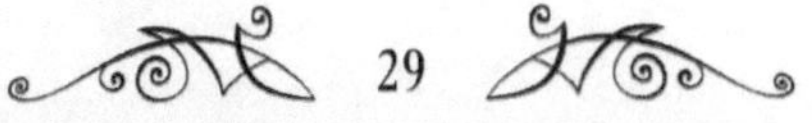

Gleaming granite countertops, stainless steel, top-of-the-line, catering-class appliances, and restored hardwood floors.

Owen opened the fridge and revealed a tray of cute, and very appetizing, sandwiches cut in triangles, scrolls, and fingers.

I popped two in my mouth at once, then picked up the whole lot on their porcelain tray. "Marianne is quite thoughtful to have prepared mobile snacks. Can we keep exploring?"

"Of course. However, Tomas is the cook, and driver. Marianne maintains the house and grounds. She's quite the skilled topiarist and does a spot of game hunting as well, if you're ever in the mood for pheasant."

"And there I was calling her old. No wonder she stays so fit."

We headed out of the kitchen. His hand remained on the small of my back, leading me as we strolled side by side along the wide corridors and I nibbled on asparagus sandwiches. There were some small living spaces, simple and yet with the same elegant gothic personality as the rest of the castle, arranged along the lower floor. We climbed the staircase upward, the steps, covered in red velour carpet, soft under my feet.

There were several bedrooms behind solid oak doors, with antique hinges and locks of wrought iron. But most exciting were the bathrooms. Huge soaking tubs, pebble-floored rain showers, and marble countertops sat under the warmth of modern heating and golden light. And we hadn't even reached the master bedroom yet.

Owen watched me explore. "Do you like it?"

"Do I like it? This oh-my-freaking-god castle I've just been gifted? Do I like it?" I repeated with my eyebrows lifted. "Let me think for a minute."

I tapped my finger gently against his firm chest, as though it helped me to ponder this difficult question. "It is beautiful. Incredible, really. Totally decadent. But also, just gothic enough to clearly be the home of a vampire," I teased, my smile a dare.

Owen's gaze became hard as he peered down at me with a cheeky sneer. In a flash, he bared his teeth and hissed.

I jumped in surprise, the tray of sandwiches falling from my grasp and shattering into a mess. Neither of us mourned the lost platter or sandwiches as Owen growled at me again, a dark lust in his eyes, and I sped off squealing and giggling down the hallway. His jacket that I'd been wearing, too large for my narrow shoulders, slipped right off and fell to the ground behind me.

My heart pounded as I raced to get away from him, all the while desperate to be caught.

He wrapped his arms around my waist just as I reached some stairs going farther up. Our momentum folded us forward and I fell on my hands and knees on the steps, his weight on my back. His mouth came down, warm across my neck, kissing hard as he ran his hands down my sides and lifted me so my ass was pressed firmly into him.

Owen's hands grasped at the bottom hem of my sundress and pushed it up my back, exposing me. He traced kisses across my bare skin, then I felt him straighten up and away from me, whip off his belt, and unbutton his pants.

He froze there, hesitating. "Wait. Um, I need …"

I knew what he meant. "No, you don't," I said. I turned myself over, wrapping my legs around his hips where he knelt just below me on the step. I pointed to the thin, firm lump under the skin of my upper arm. "Contraceptive implant, remember? I got it last month."

His fingers traced up my arm. "Of course. Sorry, keeping up with modern contraception previously hadn't been a priority for me before."

I opened my mouth to say something, but before I could his lips came back down on mine, and I forgot about technology and immortality and fertility and everything else but the feel of him in my arms, against my body. I lost myself in the sensation of my hot flesh meeting his. My dress was off over my head and flung somewhere up the stairs. The cool air brought goosebumps to my bare skin.

I showed no respect for the fine tailoring of his suit as I tore away his shirt. He slid my underpants down with reverent care, then his hands moved to undo his belt.

He stopped again. A frown creased his forehead. "Did you hear something?"

I clung to him, desire making me shake and pant, unwilling to stop. I could hear nothing but my rampant heartbeat and the kisses I spread over his skin. But the serious expression on his face cooled me down.

I listened hard. A slight creak came from somewhere. I sat up, away from Owen. He moved back too, his chest muscles becoming rigid under the light sheen of sweat. He stared down the hall we'd just run along, and his eyebrows met.

I waited but heard nothing else. "Maybe it's just the building. Aren't these old castles supposed to be all creaky and scary and stuff?"

"Maybe." The frown stayed on his face.

The creak came again.

I crossed my legs and folded my arms over my chest to cover myself, as a chill shook my whole body. I strained to hear anything to indicate what was happening.

Owen stepped quietly away from me, sneaking toward the source of the sound. I began to follow, but he held a hand up to tell me to stay. A queasy

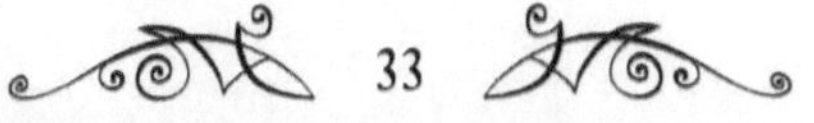

feeling grew at the base of my stomach. What was going on?

"Owen?" My whisper broke the silence, shattering it into a thousand pieces. Owen tensed, the muscles in his bare back standing in stark relief under his skin. He looked like he was poised to pounce on something, and he didn't even acknowledge that I had spoken.

Owen spoke in a low and deadly growl, "I know you're there."

The hair on the back of my neck stood up. Who was he talking to? My mouth opened to ask that question but my brain screamed at me to stay quiet. Fear froze my whole body.

The creaking came again, then I heard the definite sound of a slow, deliberate footstep. The smell of musty earth and old blood filled the hallway.

Owen tensed, his voice full of disbelief. *"Lance? Why are you here?"*

A voice came from the hallway, masculine and very deep, with a faint trace of an eastern European accent. "You've changed somehow. I smell it all over you. You smell ... human. How can this be?"

A heavy shudder rolled over my body, rippling my skin.

Owen whispered, "Kaitlyn, get dressed."

I really don't even know why he had to tell me. There was a strange man in the hallway who could smell human flesh. That should've been my first clue to get some clothes on.

I scrambled to find my dress on the stairs behind me and tugged it over my head. I didn't care about finding my underpants. Primal instinct formed words in my mind. *Just run. I have to get away from here. RUN.* But my only escape route was up. I'd been in enough slasher flicks to know what happened to people who ran upstairs. And I couldn't leave Owen.

From my angle on the stairs, I could see him, but not who he spoke to down the hall.

"You're not welcome here," Owen said through gritted teeth.

"Dear Marianne seemed happy enough to let me in on her way out." A mocking mirth filled Lance's voice.

A surge of protectiveness made my hands clench into fists. He better not have hurt Marianne.

Lance seemed to respond to my thought, but more likely to a look from Owen. "She's fine. I let her go on her way. You are who I've come to find. But to find you like this ... I hear your heartbeat. I see your undarkened eyes. I can almost taste your warmth. How? How are you human again? How is this possible?"

My legs trembled and I pressed my back to the wall of the stairwell, hiding myself from the view of the man in the hall, although I was sure he knew perfectly well I was there. And I knew, without a

shadow of a doubt, that he was a vampire.

"Leave here, Lance. I've wanted nothing to do with you for centuries, and what I am now hasn't changed that."

I groaned internally. Great. Not only did we have a vampire in the house, it was one Owen didn't get along with. I also didn't think being outright rude was the best tactic when we were frighteningly overpowered.

"Poor Owen. Now you're human, insults are all you have left to defend yourself."

I almost stepped in between their bromance-gone-wrong to tell them to cool off, but doubted it would be a smart move.

Lance said, "No, I'll be going nowhere. There is something here. Something ... delicious."

My stomach quivered and bile rose in my throat. I had no doubt that he meant me.

Air rushed by me and then on the stairs, right in front of me, stood the vampire.

Lance was older than Owen. An eternal silver fox, he had a thick mop of hair the color of bright steel, and his eyes were deep pools of black, the same as Owen's had once been before he drank from me. The dark jeans and black shirt he wore seemed too mundane for the creature he was. He had a V-shaped torso and a long, lean body, as if he'd just stepped out of an anime. A lazy smirk gave his features a roguish touch, but my body only responded to his handsome appearance as it had to Owen when I'd first seen him. With primal, animalistic fear.

I shrieked and dashed to Owen, hiding behind him.

"Don't you dare touch her," Owen growled.

Lance said, "I see nothing here but weak humans. How *ever* could you stop me?"

I gulped and pressed closer to Owen. His body was so tense that the muscles along the base of his neck had corded up, and his hands had balled into tight fists. I tried to breathe but could take in no air. I buried my face in Owen's back. I tried to think, to find an answer to Lance's teasing, rhetorical question I could slap him back with. To know we had any way of stopping him. I had nothing.

"I will kill you, Lance. Make no mistake, whatever friendship we once had is gone, and whatever ties I had to the vampire community and its laws are gone. If you lay one fang upon her, I will make you pay. She is mine. I have claimed her."

I chanced a look at Lance. His face had an almost drugged look of lust, his lips curling open with each breath, revealing sharp fangs. His gaze was on me, as though Owen had said nothing at all.

"Your claim over this delicious morsel would only mean something if you were a vampire. You've turned into a human and a fool. Maybe *I* should claim her. I must taste that blood."

"Lance, listen, there are consequences. Her blood isn't normal. It will change you," Owen warned. But I knew. It was true before, what Lance had said. Words were all we had, and they weren't working.

"You just don't want me to drink from your woman. But I will, and you will watch her blood flow into my mouth."

Owen threw his whole body at Lance.

A scream dislodged itself from my throat as they collided. Owen was larger than Lance, wider, thicker, more muscled. But that would have only given him the advantage if they were both human, or maybe even if they were both vampires. They smashed into a hall table. A vase of flowers fell, shattering with a sharp musical jangle. The scent of crushed freesias and lilies filled the air.

Owen shouted back at me, "Get to the luggage, get the blue bottle!"

I didn't know what he meant. But I ran. I couldn't do anything there. The only hope for us was for me to get away, to get a weapon. Maybe that was what the blue bottle was. Then maybe, maybe I could save Owen and myself.

The length of the hallway passed by me in a blur.

My feet slipped on something sharp. A broken piece of the sandwich platter met the sole of my right foot, slicing into it. A harsh yelp came from my throat. Pain shot upward from my foot into my ankle. My arms waved in the air as I groped for something, anything at all, for balance.

I fell so hard that my teeth clicked together and met on my tongue, bringing up the coppery taste of blood to my mouth. My head went backward, cracking against the hard marble floor.

Blackness hovered on the edges of my vision. Down the hall, Owen and Lance fought, their bodies a blur through the graying fog that tried to take me down into unconsciousness.

Lance was a vampire.

Owen was a very new human. It wasn't a fair fight at all.

Owen charged toward Lance again. Blood streamed down Owen's face, his nose likely broken.

Lance tossed him across the corridor like a wet rag. He landed with a sickening thud and didn't move.

"No! Owen!"

My hand closed around the largest shard of porcelain I could reach.

Lance came toward me, terrifyingly fast, but all the horror that I felt wasn't for myself. It was for Owen.

He lay still, an unmoving heap of bloodied flesh.

Lance stood over me, his hand tangled into my hair. He lifted me to my feet with a ripping, searing *pain as some hair tore away from my scalp.*

This was meant to be my home, my fairy tale castle, and it had become a nightmare. My home …

Lance said Marianne had let him in. Did vampires need invitations?

"I uninvite you!" I cried out.

Lance's lips quirked up, amused. "How are you with Owen, yet know so little about vampires?"

Defiantly, I stabbed the jagged piece of porcelain right at his face.

Lance snarled. He knocked the shard from my hand. He clamped down hard on my arms and I hovered there in his unrelenting grip. I had barely broken his skin, that hard, vampire skin.

But I had made him angry. I could see it all over his face. Angry, hungry, and lustful.

I panted out, "You don't want to eat me. You don't know what you're getting yourself into."

His fangs glistened, long and sharp. He inhaled my scent and growled.

Before I could say anything else his teeth were in my neck. Rough, deep, tearing. He drank in vast gulps that would take all of me. He was just as savage as Owen was the first time he drank from me, or more.

I struggled and fought, but Lance's hands held me like iron manacles. A sensation I knew too well.

The pain in my neck grew and grew. The icy yet hot sensation spread through me like lightning. Revulsion set in. That violation, that entering of my body with his teeth, that taking of something that was solely and wholly mine, my blood—it was something I had thought I would never have to feel again.

Tears ran down my face and dripped off my chin. The roaring in my ears grew louder, as though my heartbeat echoed there, the weak thumps growing slower and slower. But his frenzied devouring of me didn't slow at all.

The room spun as blood loss overwhelmed me.

Just before I faded away, a strange and terrible clarity came, briefly, with the thought that this time, I might not wake up again.

4

OWEN

ight, a faint and flickering glimmer, woke me. It got brighter and brighter with each second. With it came pain.

My eyes watered as the sting in my nose, back of my head, and shoulder all returned in force. I blinked the tears away, my eyes searching, taking in my surroundings.

Lance knelt on the floor, his eyes glazed and forehead wrinkled in confusion as he looked down. Kaitlyn lay there before him, unmoving. Even from a distance I could see her lips were blue. My heart leapt into my throat.

"What have you done? WHAT HAVE YOU DONE?" I roared.

My screams woke Lance from his stupor. He

glanced at me, frowned, then back to Kaitlyn. His pupils had lightened to a warm gray. Down one cheek, a thin, red scratch healed rapidly.

"She's alive. She's … what is she?"

"She's in hypovolemic shock, that's what she is," I hissed, crawling my way to be by her side. I ran my hands over her cold face and felt her slow heartrate. I shook her gently, called to her. She would not rouse.

Lance just stared at her, then at his own bloody hands.

"Help me. Help me save her," I begged.

Lance did nothing for a painfully long moment, and then nodded.

"There are first-aid supplies in my luggage."

Lance stood slowly, glanced at Kaitlyn again, then disappeared in a blur. I groaned, my shoulder protesting as I scooped Kaitlyn into my arms. I took her to the closest bedroom and laid her on the bed, elevating her legs.

I wasn't sure Lance would come back, but he did. He brought a bag of IV fluids, bandages, and epinephrine. All vampires who cared to keep their food alive knew how to treat blood-loss. And these days, I still kept around what I could, just in case. Easy to acquire, long shelf-life supplies only, but hopefully they would be enough. Once I was in control of my vampirism, I had always been careful not to drink so much my victims suffered from blood loss. Kaitlyn had been the first since modern medicine with whom I couldn't control myself. And I hadn't been prepared. All I'd had was coconut water. I was lucky she was tough.

I hoped she was tough enough to survive this.

Lance dumped the supplies listlessly on the bed beside Kaitlyn. I moved quickly, hanging the IV bag from a post of the bed's canopy and running the line down into one of Kaitlyn's veins. I gave her a shot of epinephrine to get her heart pumping faster again, then began bandaging her neck. Lance stood silent and still beside me the whole time.

My mind was split between doing everything I could to save Kaitlyn, and finding a sharp piece of wood to stab into Lance's heart.

Kaitlyn stirred. The smallest movement, her blue lips parted.

Lance turned away.

"Lance," I started, not sure what to say next.

He glanced back over his shoulder, his face a scary mix of emotions. Then he walked out, closing the door behind him.

I heard the click of the lock.

I cursed him. And I cursed myself for ever knowing him, for ever being a vampire, for ever being part of that bloody world. For everything Kaitlyn has suffered because of it, and was likely to yet.

But when we got free from this room, I would

have my revenge on Lance. If I could only get to my luggage and get the Nemexia, or to the hidden vault where I kept my even deadlier weapon. I still had my secrets.

It felt like hours I knelt beside that bed as though in prayer, watching Kaitlyn for more signs of life, waiting for her to come back to me.

Then I stood, pacing the room in long, thumping strides, rage building on hopelessness.

It was a long time before Kaitlyn's voice, soft and rough, reached me. "You're not dead."

I raced to her side. "No. I'm still here, and so are you."

She tried to sit up. I put my hand on her shoulder and gently pressed her back. "Don't. You lost a lot of blood, and you really need to stay lying down."

Her eyes drifted closed. "I thought he killed you," she breathed out.

Tears ran down the side of her face, and while her eyes were still closed, I let just one of my own fall. We were alive, and as long as we were, we could work the rest of this mess out together.

I wiped my thumb across her temple, wiping away the tears. "That makes us even then. I thought he'd killed you as well."

"I think it was a really close thing there for a second. It felt like he was never going to stop."

I looked back at the locked door. "But he did."

Her hands sought out mine, her fingers chilled and shivering. "Where is he now?"

"He let me carry you in here. But he's locked us in."

"Ugh," she groaned. "You know I hate being a crab."

I frowned. Maybe she wasn't as lucid as I'd thought. The blood loss must have her confused.

"I mean," she continued with a *don't look at me like I'm crazy* expression. "How you once explained how people yank their legs off, toss them back into the ocean and let them grow new ones only to take them out again and snap off another one. I don't like feeling like a crab. Sure, this Lance guy stopped now, but maybe he just stopped so that he could save me for later."

My face fell. That was exactly what I'd done to her. When I'd first compared her to a crab it was to explain that she was only food to me, nothing more. As though *she* were the fool for not being able to understand her role.

"I won't let that happen. Not again."

"Then how do we get out of here?" she asked.

I surveyed the space we'd ended up in. It was the corner room, built into a tower. The ceiling was incredibly high, rising to form a conical point. There were a few windows, slim slits with stained glass that were fixed in place, and too narrow to fit through anyway. We were on a four-poster bed, designed to look old, but quite modern with a quality mattress.

Being a guestroom, it was devoid of any personal effects or decoration. The adjoining bathroom had the most basic toiletries, and no way of escape.

The bedroom door was thick, heavy wood. The old-fashioned two-way lock required a key that could be used on either side. The kind of lock where you could slide a piece of paper under the door and push the key out onto, if you were lucky enough that the key was left in the other side, and you had paper, and something to push the key through with. Lance had taken the key from the inside where it was normally kept. I looked through the keyhole, but he hadn't left the key in. I wasn't surprised. It was the oldest trick in the book, and he was just as old.

Kaitlyn looked around too, taking in the room first and then the IV line to her arm.

"Why do you think he stopped?"

"Given the look of utter horror on his face, I imagine the same thing happened to him that happened to me when I drank from you. I think your blood changed him."

"Do you think he's human now? He drank a lot."

I shook my head. A strange jealousy grew within me, that another vampire could taste Kaitlyn, could be changed by her. "No. He drank a lot, but the truth is, I drank much the same amount from you that first time too. While it changed my emotions immediately, it didn't make me human then. It took more … much more." My voice cracked, and I looked away, studying the IV line and avoiding Kaitlyn's eyes.

"Owen." Kaitlyn's voice grew stern. "I forgave you for that. But my forgiving you doesn't mean it didn't happen. We can't spend the rest of our lives tap dancing around the subject, and I'm not willing to hate you for it, because it wasn't you. You are no longer that monster. But you have to stop hating yourself too. I can't do that for you."

"I know. The things I did when I was a vampire … I may have been a different person then, a different creature, but I still did those things. I will always have remorse and regret, and I don't think that's a bad thing. I think for me to stay human I need those feelings."

Kaitlyn smiled up at me. Her eyelids fluttered, and I knew staying awake, and talking, were a struggle for her.

"You should rest. Sleep if you can. Recover while I find a way for us to get out of here, so you have your strength when the time comes."

"Tell me about Lance, how you know him," she said in a whisper. "Knowledge is pretty much the only power we have right now."

"Lance … He was my best friend, once. Older than me, both in human and vampire age, but he's never told me how much older. When I was free of Adelle,

and trying to find my way, he was my mentor."

Kaitlyn lay still. Her hands squeezed mine lightly.

"All those years ago, Lance was a different type of being. He used to get angry at me for not always making the moral choice. He taught me that although we … *they* do not have the same compunctions or empathy as humans, that doesn't mean you can't use logic to decide which course is the better moral option.

"Lance was always on the side of doing the right thing. The thing that would cause the least harm to humans. Vampires may see humans as food, but you can still treat your food well before you devour it."

I paused for a long moment. Kaitlyn's breathing was steady, and deep. I smiled, knowing she'd recover. She was a survivor. I thought she'd fallen asleep when she squeezed my hand again.

"So, what happened?"

"I'm not sure exactly. Something did happen though. He changed, grew cynical, hateful, outright violent toward humans. I always wondered if perhaps it wasn't so much a case of him being cynical as it was a case of him becoming bored. Tired of trying to do the right thing when it went against his nature. You can't live as long as him and not get bored."

"Sure. I get bored occasionally, and I've hardly lived at all."

I looked at her face, her eyes still closed, but a cheeky smile cracked her lips, which had regained some color. Still so young, so few years she'd had to experience this world, this life. "I never should have brought you here. I never should have returned to this place from my past. I should have sold it and moved on, buried Owen Raine completely. I am so sorry."

Her eyes opened then, reprimanding me with a look for my expression of guilt. "If it didn't happen now, here, this was likely to happen anyway. Wasn't it?"

I couldn't answer. It had been my biggest fear every moment since my Strawberry had walked free of the home I'd held her captive in.

"Me and my damned tasty blood. It's why you had me followed, after you set me free. It's why you hired bodyguards for me while I was on set. I thought you were just being protective. I thought maybe, maybe chances of coming across another vampire were low."

"Not low enough. The perfume I gave you, it was for your protection too. It was based on Nemexia, or corpse flower, a fragrance that can knock out a vampire. Things like holy water are a myth, but Nemexia, wormwood, and a few other botanical extracts can be quite effective. I have some more of the perfume in my luggage, if we can somehow get to it."

"Why didn't you tell me? I would have worn it always if I'd known."

"I should have. I should have told you all these

things, but I didn't want you to always be scared. I wanted you to have nothing to do with that world." I shook my head slowly. *I wanted to protect her from all of this. From the truth of what is out there.*

"How many ..." Her voice choked off and started again. "How many vampires are there out there? I mean, really, how many could there be?"

I couldn't lie anymore. "Tens of thousands. Hundreds of thousands. Maybe millions. A whole society, all across the world. One with a long and bloody history, with its own standards and laws. One with every facet of vampire character. Those who follow the law. Those who follow a spiritual path. Solitary ones, and those who form communities. Those who only kill to eat. Those who let their food live. Those who kill for pleasure. A world I wanted to keep you free from, and failed."

Kaitlyn looked away. She stared at the wall, her lips parted. Fresh tears pooled in her eyes.

A faint opalescence hung in the corners of the windows; a tinge of light that said dawn would come soon. A dawn I could only see because of her. She had changed me. Maybe she could change Lance as well. Maybe we still had hope.

"What do you think will happen to Lance now he has had my blood? I mean, can we use him having drunk my blood to our advantage? If he had enough, maybe he gained some ... you know, some feelings.

Perhaps we could work on those feelings to try to get him to release us."

"I was thinking the same thing."

It was, in a way, what she'd done to me. I know she'd played on my growing feelings as her blood changed me. I couldn't blame her; she was just trying to stay alive. Now, I found myself questioning whether I'd be able to watch her seduce Lance in the same way if it meant her living. I didn't want to answer. I wanted the inhuman strength and lack of remorse I once had back so I could rip Lance to shreds.

The pearly glow in the windows was diffused by a golden-rose-colored blush. I stared at it.

Kaitlyn did too. "Help me up."

"Why?"

"The sun's rising," she said softly. "I want to see it, and so do you."

I did. I needed to see the sun, to hold onto my humanity and all it meant.

The IV was empty, so I removed it from her arm. I helped Kaitlyn from the bed and then carried her to one of the windows. I held her as I settled into the window seat, cradling her, and we stared out through the thick glass.

The view was magnificent from that room. A view I had never been able to enjoy until now, my first time in this place as a human. The high and jagged peaks of the mountains lit up and glowed, as though

someone had set them on fire. The sun, coming up between two peaks, hung there, framed by the stark rocks, a glowing orb whose color changed from rose to carnelian to beautiful gold. Little tendrils of color hit the sky, and those fingers stretched and raced across the heavens, sending the blackness of night fleeing before their reach.

The sun escaped the cage of the peaks and rose higher. The trees took on distinct shapes. The greenery of the pines stood in stark relief to the black rock. The sky lightened, and lightened again.

My head dropped as exhaustion came.

Kaitlyn sighed. "I know it should come as no surprise, but I'm starving. I should have pocketed some of the sandwiches instead of trying to stick Lance in the face with a broken plate. That would've been the smart plan."

An unexpected laugh coughed out of me. "I was wondering how he got that scratch."

I cuddled her closer. The thought of food made my stomach growl loudly, and Kaitlyn giggled.

She snuggled into my body. "I could really go for some outrageously cheesy pizza, and maybe a few garlic knots. Some creamy sauce for dipping, and extra—"

"Stop. I'm going to die if you don't."

She grinned.

I kissed her forehead. There was some small comfort

in the shared misery that was being hungry. Being hungry meant being alive, and we were, together.

The sun crept farther into the room, spilling broad bands of light across us and the floor. My eyes closed and I drifted off, Kaitlyn's arms around me, and the future hanging menacing and uncertain around both of us.

5

KAITLYN

I slept like the dead. Or at least the near dead, which I was sure I literally was.

Sleeping the whole day away felt like a waste. But I'd done this dance before. I knew what it was like being held captive by a vampire and drunk nearly dry. Our chances of escape were low, and even lower while I was still so weak from blood loss.

At some point, Owen had moved us back to the bed. He lay curled around me, protective, and warm. A few times through the day, I was woken by him as he got up and paced the room, tested exits, searched the bathroom, or tried to break the side-table into pointy stakes. Unsuccessfully.

I let myself sleep. Even the sound of wooden furniture being flung against the stone walls wasn't

enough to keep my eyelids open. I hovered between consciousness and the void of exhausted slumber, noticing what happened around me in a dreamlike way.

Owen returned to bed and laid beside me.

Night returned, darkening the room.

The steady creak of the door opening echoed around us.

Owen's body tensed against mine.

I woke fully, galvanized by fresh terror and the will to fight.

Owen sat up, shielding my body with his as Lance entered the room.

He flicked the light switch. His skin was a warmer tone, his irises slightly brighter than before. His expression hadn't warmed or brightened though. It was hard, thoughtful, but angry.

His hands twitched. "It's her blood, isn't it? How you became human?"

Owen shook his head. "You're mistaken. There is nothing special about her blood."

Lance laughed heartily. "Boldfaced, and ridiculous lies. It's too late to try to hide it now. There is something very special, and very delicious about her blood."

I cringed. My blood was like potato crisps. Once you slurped you couldn't stop. He was going to keep me just as Owen had. Owen had fought hard against taking more of my blood, but his willpower had faded before it every single time. I really had to get my hands on that vampire repellent perfume. I really wished Owen had told me about it before. Did he think I was too weak to know these things? He should have known better.

Owen was up off the bed. Without his shirt, I could see every muscle in his chest ripple and strain in anger. "Don't even think about biting her again. You won't get another drop of her blood. I will kill you first."

Lance remained amused. "I don't want another drop of that blood."

My jaw dropped.

"Have I hurt your feelings? Thought you were too tasty to deny?" Lance asked.

I broke eye contact. I did think that. I didn't know whether to be upset or relieved.

"You're delicious, sweetheart, but so is chocolate. It is possible to say no to chocolate."

"Says you," I muttered. Chocolate from some four-or-more hundred years ago had no chance of comparing to modern chocolate. He had *no idea.*

"Especially if you know it's bad for your health," he said.

I looked him in the eye again, trying to gauge his current motivations. He seemed serious. He had no interest in my blood.

The thought chilled me. I'd always believed Owen treated me as he did when he was a vampire because

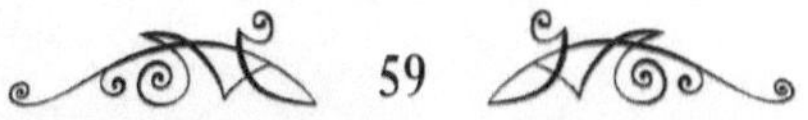

he literally couldn't resist. That the monstrous part of him had an unstoppable thirst for my blood.

But he could have stopped. Lance was choosing to stop.

The truth was, Owen chose to keep feeding from me. To keep me prisoner. Because he wanted to, and he could.

Lance had more information to make his choice. He knew the consequences of continuing to drink my blood. Maybe if he didn't know that, like Owen hadn't, he'd make a different choice. But still, I knew now that it was, indeed, a choice.

Owen sat back beside me on the bed and put his arm around me protectively. I had the strange urge to shy away from him.

He's different now. He's human now. He's not the monster that chose to keep me as food—he's the human who set me free. I tried to remind myself of all those things, but the lines felt too blurry and confused right now.

Owen's body softened, shoulders dropping. His whole posture changed from aggressive to submissive, but the small muscle twitching in his jaw told me the effort he put into making that switch. He pleaded, "Old friend, let us go. Don't get involved in what her blood could mean. Forget you saw me like this. Forget her."

Lance nodded, but just as my hopes rose, they fell again.

"I will let you go. Only I cannot free you entirely. What she's done, what you are—you can't keep this hidden."

Lance looked back at the open doorway and said, "I had to tell the council what has happened to you, and to me. You shouldn't have come here, Owen—not with nothing but human in your veins. Had I not found you, they would have scented you out fast enough. They were already looking for you anyway, with your suspicious attempt to disappear."

That's when I realized we weren't alone. I saw them moving, but didn't hear a sound, as two people—presumably vampires—dressed entirely in black came in to stand behind Lance. Their clothing matched, a uniform maybe, but more ninja-like than soldier. Long pants and full-length sleeves in flowing black silk, cowls that covered their head except their black eyes, and thick, black armor protecting just their neck and chest.

I peeked up at Owen's face. His jaw was tight. "I gave them no reason to watch for me. I was nothing to the vampire world, their politics. I never broke their laws."

Lance raised his gray eyebrows to that comment. "Whatever you may or may not have done in the past, you were a long-lived and wealthy member of both vampire and human society. Trying to make all that disappear was a mistake. Of course, they

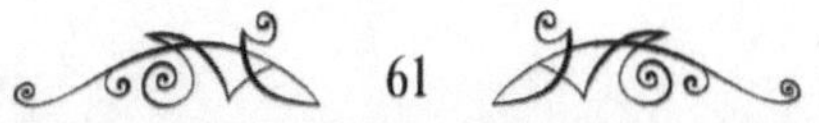

would look into it. Of course, *I* would look into it. We may not have been friends for a good century, but I was curious what happened to you. I had to look for you. Why do you think I'm here?"

"And now they know where I am, and what I am. Thanks to you," Owen growled.

Lance's shoulders lifted, then dropped. His hands opened and closed. A confused look crossed his face as he glanced at the silent black warriors flanking him. "It's out of my hands. You have been invited to the estate of the Synedrion."

Owen's eyes narrowed. A red flush of blood spread along his cheeks and forehead. "You mean we are to be taken there. That is no invitation, and you know it. Don't try to dress it up as one."

I had no idea what the Synedrion was, but it didn't sound good at all. It sounded downright terrifying in fact, as did the mention of a vampire council. I had never imagined vampires to be so organized. Then again, I'd imagined that we'd be able to avoid vampires for the rest of our lives. I clearly didn't know anything about vampires.

Lance turned away from us. "Get up. You have thirty minutes before we go. I wouldn't try anything. Joss and Ash here have been sent to make sure you both arrive at the Synedrion estate, alive."

He left the room. Left us to the cold stare of our two new jailers.

Remortality

I stood beside Owen. He pulled me under his arm and whispered, "They are Ebonguard. Vampires, but you don't have to worry about them coming after you, unless those are their orders. If their orders are to get us to the Synedrion alive, that's what is going to happen."

"And that's just the tip of the explanation iceberg I need right now. I know enough to tell we're in deep trouble. I'm going to need you to catch me up on the rest."

Owen nodded. "Come on. We need to do what they say, for now. We have little hope against a regular vampire. Let alone an Ebonguard."

I shivered. I hated being helpless. Head on confrontation would get us nowhere. We just had to wait for an opening, a chance, and there wasn't one now.

My first step forward almost dropped me to the ground. I hadn't realized how weak I still was. Owen caught me and supported me through to the adjoining bathroom. We weren't allowed to close the door. We showered quickly and at the same time. Under other circumstances that would have been sexy. Instead, it was frightening and tense. I carefully washed away the dried blood around my neck. The warm water helped bring my body back from the deathly cold I'd been feeling, but it didn't stop the shakes.

One of the Ebonguard had brought our suitcases

up into the room while we showered. It seemed like a thoughtful, almost human gesture. They probably just wanted to hurry us along though.

I met Owen's glance with the same look of hope when we saw our cases, mine still unopened from our arrival the day before, Owen's riffled through for the first-aid supplies. Before we could reach them though, one Ebonguard unzipped and worked through each bag, their hands flashing with speed as they searched. I held my breath, and almost groaned it out when the Ebonguard held up a tiny blue vial. Lance must have told them about it.

And buh-bye, there went that plan.

We weren't left alone to dress, so Owen blocked me as best he could from the view of our guards. I dug out some purple fleece tights and a chunky-knit, ivory sweater dress. I didn't care who we were seeing or how I should dress for the occasion. I needed comfort clothes right now. Owen put on navy-blue suit pants and a pale gray t-shirt. We both grabbed our warmest coats and zippered up our luggage which was taken away again by one of our ninja-like companions.

Owen checked his watch. We had less than ten minutes, so headed quickly to the kitchen. I could have eaten a twelve-course degustation with a few large pizzas on the side. But we didn't have time for much more than a scant meal, whatever we could grab. We scarfed down thickly sliced creamy brie on crusty sour-dough bread, and a couple of cups of hot, strong coffee. There was a bowl of fresh fruit, and I grabbed an apple for the road. I tried to slip a steak knife into my pocket too, but an Ebonguard snatched it back from me with a chiding shake of their head.

The thundering hum of a helicopter landing out the front marked the end of our stay.

"Time to go," said one of the guards. I was stunned to hear a woman's voice. The cowl, armor, and loose uniform hid most of their body shape. Looking again, I supposed it wasn't too unclear it was a female form. Maybe both of them could be. The names Joss and Ash could go either way.

I downed the last sip of my coffee and we were led outside.

Black shadows crept around the statues on the lawn and clung to every corner of the grounds. We were loaded into the helicopter, and I was glad to see our luggage coming with us. A small sign that they didn't intend to kill us right away. That maybe we really were going to be treated like guests rather than prisoners. Joss and Ash took the seat opposite us, our knees touching theirs in the small space.

Lance was in the front, across from the pilot, another Ebonguard.

When he saw we were all in, he said something inaudible. He and the pilot wore headsets that they

could speak to each other through, but the roar of the engine and blades was all I could hear. I tried to say something to Owen, but even my own voice was only a dull hum.

I wanted to ask so many questions. Who were the vampires we were being forced to go see? And where were we being taken? What would they do to us? Would they kill us? Would they see my blood as a threat to their very nature? Or as a savior?

There was no way to know.

The helicopter rocked on its feet as it lifted from the ground. We bobbed about in the air, the sensation of flight so much different than in a plane. Then the pressure of acceleration pushed me back into the seat, and the details of the world below us vanished into black.

I stared out the window, my hand clutched in Owen's, and tried to just breathe.

I looked over at him. He gazed back at me.

I mouthed, *"I love you."*

He kissed my forehead in return.

Far below, small towns and cities passed by beneath us, their lights like glittering streams in the darkness.

We continued onward through the gloomy night, through a darkness as deep but not nearly as restful as the grave.

6

KAITLYN

I checked my phone during the trip. The Ebonguard kept an eye on me, although didn't try to take it off me. There was no reception as we flew anyway, even if I thought I could call anyone for help. I could just imagine how that call to 911 would go.

"Hi, what's your emergency?"

"Well, I've been kidnapped by vampire ninjas and I'm in a helicopter who-knows-the-fuck-where."

Even if emergency services could help, I didn't know what country we were in at this point. I didn't have enough reception to send a message or get online. I ended up playing a tower defense game, just to kill time and take my mind off the anxiety that swirled as fast as the helicopter blades. I ate the apple I brought along, sharing with Owen bite for bite, and wished I'd pocketed the whole fruit bowl, and some chocolate bars, and the coffee machine.

We'd been in the air for about two hours when we finally descended to land. I was ready to be on solid ground again; the whir of the helicopter felt embedded in my bones like a strange vibrating sickness. It worsened the fear I already felt about this enforced invitation into the vampire world.

The helicopter went down, down, as though descending into the pits of hell. Darkness rose on either side of us as we flew low between two mountain ranges, deeper into a valley where even the stars and moon above seemed out of sight.

Then light flared around us as we reached the flood-lit landing pad. Vampires may have been creatures of the night, but they didn't seem averse to having well-lit spaces.

The helicopter landed with the crunch of gravel underneath and the whump, whump, whump of the blades winding down.

"We're here," Owen said, and squeezed my hand. Hearing his voice was like I'd been deaf and suddenly learned to hear again. He spoke low, although I imagined the vampires around us could hear him anyway. Did they have super-hearing? I added that to my list of vampire information I needed.

"Where *is* here?" I whispered back. My voice didn't want to work.

"Romania. Umbravallis, the Valley of Shadow."

"Cheery," I said.

Owen rushed his words, as though trying to catch up on what he hadn't been able to tell me during our flight. "It is home to the Synedrion, a powerful vampire council who oversee a large vampire community, and imagine themselves the rulers of all vampires. Umbravallis is a valley so deep it only gets direct sunlight in summertime. This is where vampires go when they prefer to live only amongst their own kind, by their own rules, rather than living hidden alongside humans. There is a town, a number of private estates, and the estate of the Synedrion."

"Great. So, it's Vampireland. We're in Vampireland. Are we the only humans here?"

Owen's expression became grim. "No. There will be thralls too. Food sources, slaves, some willing victims, some not."

I shuddered at the thought.

The Ebonguard on my right slid the helicopter door open. Outside lay a barren, rocky landscape, as though we'd just landed on the moon. Nothing seemed alive out there. A soft wind blew through the night, bringing the earthy scent of dust and dryness.

We were ushered out almost politely and loaded into an awaiting car. Joss and Ash got in the back with us. The divider between the back and front

was clear glass, and Lance got in the driver's seat. He tapped at the dash of touch screens and the car moved without any further action from him. Driverless technology. So the vamps here were up on modern luxuries and had the money for it too. A self-driving car would be very handy if you had to black out every window.

The road was smooth and well-made, despite the sharp, craterous landscape around us. We glided along, soon passing wider areas filled with walled estates and immaculate mansions. Not many gardens though. Only a few misshapen plants grew here with so little sunlight: potted plants of varieties I'd never seen, and a few leafless, tortured trees. Estate grounds were mostly paved, decorated with fountains and statues. One we passed had fake trees in colors of gold and silver. And all those homes had vampires inside.

"We're going to be seeing more vampires, lots of vampires. This doesn't feel safe at all. What if one decides my blood is just too delicious?" I looked to Owen for assurance, but Ash, or Joss, whichever one it was, beat him to the answer.

"That's why we are here. To ensure your safety. You will be under guard for your protection throughout your stay."

For my protection and imprisonment, I wanted to argue. But didn't. I was starting to learn to keep my mouth shut. Sometimes.

Joss and Ash were all business, and appeared to have no interest in my blood, which comforted me a little. Neither did Lance, now he knew what it did. That didn't mean I was safe. The Synedrion wanted to see us because of my blood and what it was reported to do.

Once they'd seen for themselves … best possible outcome? They could like the idea of having the choice to go human again and we become lab rats. Worst possible outcome? The end.

I couldn't see any way out of this, but if these vampires could be reasoned with, I was preparing myself to do as much reasoning as possible. Vampires could be intelligent, and they even had emotions of a sort. They just lacked empathy. I imagined myself about to deal with a room full of sociopaths. Could be a bit like some days in Hollywood.

We passed through a small town. Historic buildings mixed with occasional modern shops and apartment towers, the roads all lit with elegant streetlights designed like hanging bell-flowers. People … *vampires* moved about, as though it were a normal day, shopping, chatting, drinking at a café. Probably not coffee though. I had the oddest sensation, the strangest little thought that this was all some fantastical movie set and that at any minute the director would yell "cut," the lights would go up, and there would be normalcy just beyond

the car's closed doors and windows.

I blinked hard and then bit my lip. The slight pain grounded me, snapped me out of the disorientation and disassociation that I had been floating toward. I knew how dangerous that was, and just how seductive. I had to keep my wits about me no matter how much I would rather pretend this was all some dream that would blow away the moment I awakened.

My eyes widened as we drove into the largest cavern I had ever seen. The road went right in, lined with those same ornate streetlights. Floodlights lit the cave, showing off the impressive limestone falls, columns, and stalagmites and stalactites, all old-bone yellow, like the cave had its own skeleton and teeth.

We passed through massive iron gates, onwards toward a palace that had been built of the same stone that surrounded it, up against the back of the cave itself. Three stories in height, the palace was lined with columns cut from dripping limestone, and elegant arched windows that shone brightly from within, accentuating their pointed gothic style.

The circular entrance drive looped around a huge fountain created from a spiral-shaped limestone column. Parked cars crowded the front of the building. I imagined that gossip had already spread, and hundreds of black eyes looked down from the windows to see the vampire turned human and the woman who had made that happen.

We pulled up amongst the row of cars. A blank and silent human came to take our bags. Her pale, blue eyes held no expression, and the modern, gray housekeeping uniform she wore hung loose over her malnourished frame. She didn't have the same stink of crazy about her that Loretta had had. I wanted to reach out to her, shake her from her slavery and see her run free, but she ignored me entirely.

Drips from the fountain plinked melodically, but its music was offset by the shriek and chatter of bats in the cave ceiling high above.

Joss and Ash led the way inside. Owen's arm wrapped around me but brought me no comfort. Lance walked ahead, then dropped back to be beside us.

He opened his mouth, hesitating for a moment before he actually spoke, "If it's worth anything, I'm sorry about this. Just after drinking your blood, I was flooded with feelings, with anger and confusion at so many things. Mostly at myself. I contacted the Synedrion before I had the clarity I have now. Before I considered what it could mean. For you, Kaitlyn and Owen, and for all of us. I fear I've made a mistake."

He seemed sincere, almost sad. His skin tone had barely anything left of the warmth it had held after drinking from me, and his eyes were pure black again. But here he was, expressing regret.

"A mistake?" Owen grunted. "You've doomed us."

Lance's eyebrows furrowed, then he rolled his eyes, as though chasing that expression away. "You're over-reacting. I'm sure the Synedrion will treat you well."

Owen snorted in disagreement.

"It's done now. What are you going to do to help keep us alive if they don't treat us well?" I challenged.

Lance's head bowed. "I'm not sure what your experience with vampires has been like in the past, but we can be perfectly reasonable. Some may see your blood and what it can do as an offense to our kind, but I'm sure they will be a minority. Having tasted it … having known these human feelings again, even if they fade from me and I never drink from you a second time, you've changed me. I used to be a better man in the past. I had forgotten those emotions. I had forgotten the reasons why. But I've been reminded."

He looked Owen in the eyes then. "I want to be that better man again. I don't see how that can be a bad thing."

Owen held his gaze and nodded his approval.

Yay. A new vampire friend, I thought, not without sarcasm. If it takes every single vampire on Earth drinking from me to turn them to my side, that might be a bit much.

We stepped into a three-story-high entry hall hung with two rows of brightly lit crystal chandeliers. Not the black wrought-iron, filled-with-bright-red-candles cliché I'd been expecting. Whoever these vampires were, they had beautiful taste.

"It's all so bright," I said.

"Expecting it to be dark and gloomy?" Lance said, raising a silver brow. "Vampires see well in the dark, but only a dull, black and white view of the world. Color and warmth is still appreciated, even if it's not necessary."

A huge casual area, almost like you'd find in a hotel lobby or bar, lay beyond the entry hall. Black satin and rich leather armchairs filled the generous space.

You know what else filled that space? Vampires. Vampires filled that space.

As we walked in, almost every one of them paused to stare at us. Some bared their fangs. Others sneered and whispered to each other.

My feet were working on their own, walking backwards. An irrepressible fear had taken over my body and I had to get out of there. It's not safe for a lamb to be in a place with so many wolves. Every instinct I had screamed *GET OUT!*

One of the Ebonguard grabbed me by the shoulder, halting my progress. "You are safe," he said, simply. *He.* The distinction between him and the female Ebonguard shocked me out of the fight-or-flight instinct. I still didn't know which was Joss and which was Ash though.

Owen and Lance took their positions on either side of me again. My small entourage improved my spirits, and I faced the room again.

The vampires stared at us like we were the new kids at school. Scattered between them, dozens of human thralls moved about. Some fawned over their vampire masters, but in a dull, drug-hazed way. Others were being fed on, right there in the open, their faces blank to the pain. Some stood motionless simply awaiting their next command. I wanted to help them, but didn't even know how to help myself.

A vampire with slick black hair and a carefully trimmed beard suddenly appeared before us. His hand was outstretched to grab Owen, but was held mid-air by the male Ebonguard. I hadn't even seen any of it happen. One moment we were walking, the next, there he was.

The female Ebonguard stepped forward. "These guests are under the protection of the Synedrion."

They stood like that for a moment, sizing each other up. Long enough for me to take in the situation, before the black-haired vampire submitted and backed off a step.

I heard Owen let out a long, slow breath. "Dante. Haven't seen you since—"

"Since Adelle," Dante spat back at him. "Since you killed her."

I raised an eyebrow. I knew the story of Adelle.

Owen had told me how vampires weren't allowed to kill each other, and that a cursed ring had found its way to Adelle. Seemed Dante had heard a different story.

"You know that's not true," Owen said. "I was cleared of any suspicion regarding her death."

Lance flicked his chin up. "Bugger off, Dante. We've got no time for your drama."

Dante grunted. He leaned in dangerously close to Owen, hissing in his ear, "I was there when she died. She hid me from you, knowing how jealous you were, how you'd killed her other lovers in the past. I don't know how you did it, but I saw you take something from the dust you turned her to, and one day I will prove your guilt."

My eyes widened. Before I could fully process what Dante had said, a tall female vampire stepped up behind him. She placed her French-tipped fingernails lightly on Dante's shoulder. His lips twitched closed as he turned to her. Silky blond hair fell around her moon-like face.

She smiled through lips painted a perfectly glossy nude-pink. "Playing nice, Dante?"

His response was to growl and stalk away.

Owen greeted the woman with a formal embrace and European-style double-cheek kiss. "Night's greetings, Niamh."

"To you too." She looked him over and grimaced. "It looks like you've done it this time." She leaned close

again and took a sniff of him. A spike of jealousy hit hard. Vampire or no, how dare she sniff my man like that?

In a voice filled with wonder, she said, "It's true. You … you changed back to human!" A blood tear ran down her face. Her hands shook.

My own lips parted. I didn't know vampires could cry, that they could feel much other than hunger. There was something so powerful about that single tear of blood. I wondered if it were a happy tear, or a tear of mourning.

"Night's greetings, Niamh." Lance kissed her in the same way Owen had. I wondered if all vampires knew each other, or if this was a select circle, the vampire upper-class, which I could imagine Owen would have at some point been part of.

Then Niamh's gaze fell on me. I smiled, thinking for a moment to try to win her over. But her nostrils flared and her tongue swiped across her bared fangs. Her voice was thick. "Well, hello there. I was warned you would smell delicious." Her eyes darted briefly to Joss and Ash standing by me. She blinked and offered a polite smile. "Come. I'm to show you to your accommodations."

Niamh led us out. I tried to catch Owen's eye with a WTF expression, but it was like he was avoiding looking at me.

The opulence of the palace we walked through

rivalled that of Versailles. Thralls hurried about their tasks, none of them speaking a word to anyone. The sound of music, baroque and stringed, drifted from somewhere. Many vampires we passed eyed us with unhidden repulsion.

"Ignore them," Niamh said. "It's natural some will see Owen's change as an abomination. Some simply see him as a curiosity. But there are some who see him as something else entirely, a hope long ago lost."

Owen didn't react when a male vampire, wearing a well-tailored black suit with a dark dress shirt, paused, hissed, and raced away from us like we were carrying the plague.

Well, okay, maybe I was carrying some kind of vampire changing plague, but Owen wasn't.

Or was he? He didn't have the yummy scent I apparently had, but we had no experience yet with a vampire drinking from him. I was sure this would be something else the vampires here would want to know, maybe even to test.

Niamh stopped at a door, smiled, and punched in some numbers on a keypad so fast her fingers were a blur. The door clicked open.

Lance bowed very slightly. "I'll see you again soon," he said. Clearly being our friend didn't mean being trapped in our "accommodations" with us.

"You'll have some time to rest before the council meet. You'll be provided with food and medical aid

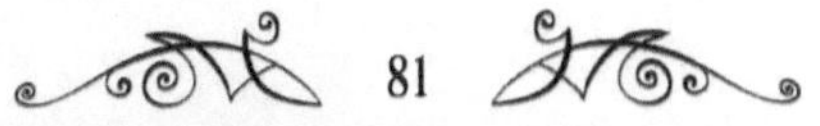

shortly. I must also ask now that you surrender your phones and any other connected devices to us."

We both reluctantly handed over our phones.

"There is a laptop in their luggage as well," said the male Ebonguard.

Niamh narrowed her eyes at us, and Owen just shrugged. Hey, couldn't blame him for not mentioning it, right?

The laptop was collected by one of the Ebonguard, then Niamh stood back from the door and waved her arm for us to enter.

Owen ushered me inside and the door shut, the click of the lock unmistakable. My shoulders tensed. *I'm getting real tired of vampires locking me up.*

"At least the room's nice," Owen said.

I rolled my eyes. A pretty prison was still a prison, but I could imagine a rat-infested, muddy, medieval dungeon would be a lot worse. I guessed I was grateful for that.

"Owen, you do know they could decide to eat the both of us at any moment."

"I do."

I saw real pain written on his face then, torment showing in the wet gloss of his eyes and twitch of his jaw.

"I ... I have never wished so much to be a vampire before. If I still was, we wouldn't be here. Lance wouldn't have dared to take your blood back at the castle, as it was claimed as mine."

"I get that he wouldn't have done it because … I don't know, maybe stealing another vampire's blood vessel is like the human version of double-dipping chips or something, but you know I prefer you as a human. Mostly because I didn't much care for you sucking my blood."

Owen's shoulders dropped lower. His voice was a throaty growl. "You're still my Strawberry. The one thing I can't live without. I wish I still had the strength to protect you."

My heart beat a little faster. I loved him so much, and I hated to see him so torn about being human. I hated it, and the guilt that crept over me at that helplessness he felt due to being human, a state I caused him to be. Being human was a weakness we shared now, and that weakness might see one, or both, of us dead.

"I can't live without you either." My hand grazed his shoulder. I turned to him, and my mouth caught his.

The kiss was long and lingering. My body arched into his and he wrapped me tightly in his arms. My eyelids fell closed as I clung desperately to him. I still reacted to him with such a primal, fierce longing. My cheeks flushed and hands roamed. I wanted him so badly that I shook with the heady mix of desire and fear.

There was a knock on the door, and we both

tensed. The door opened and a thrall entered, bearing a tray of food hidden under silver domed lids. Joss and Ash stood outside the door, and had probably been there the whole time. The food was placed down on a table and the thrall left as a new vampire arrived. He carried an old-fashioned doctor's bag, but was gangly and looked too young to be a doctor. With vampires, though, visual age meant nothing.

Joss or Ash, I still didn't know which was which, followed him in, closing the door behind them.

"So, are you a human doctor or a vampire doctor?" I asked.

"I'm a vampire doctor to humans. Vampires generally have no need for doctors, but their thralls do," he said, his voice blunt.

He put his bag down on the table next to the food, and clicked it open.

"Quite the oddity, you two," he said, failing to introduce himself again. Doctor Vampire pulled a modern-looking blood-pressure monitor from his bag and took my arm without even asking.

"Um, excuse me?"

He didn't react to my objection either as he continued checking me over, flashing a light in my eyes, cleaning and redressing the wound on my neck, and injecting me with something. I looked to Owen in alarm.

"Probably antibiotics, for the risk of infection,"

he offered.

"Blood-loss medication," the doctor corrected. He didn't bother with more details.

Apparently finished with me, he checked Owen's vitals as well. He noted all down on a slim tablet computer, then just like that, packed away his gear.

"Eat the food. Drink lots of liquids," he ordered.

I realized that was probably how he was used to treating humans, if thralls were his main customers. Bedside manner from a creature with no empathy who only treated brainwashed slaves was probably too much to ask.

Then he left, the Ebonguard at the door following him out and giving us some privacy again.

"Food it is then," I said.

Owen opened the room service, to reveal two bowls of a very thick, unappealing gray stew and glasses of room-temperature water.

"Wow. I guess human food isn't a big priority around here."

"It is dull, but nutritious, full of iron. It is what the thralls eat."

I sighed.

We ate in silence. My mind swirled like a tornado, but instead of dust and debris it was filled with fears and all the things I'd learned so quickly about vampires. I had so much I wanted to ask Owen, but the darker thoughts, the doubts, started creeping in.

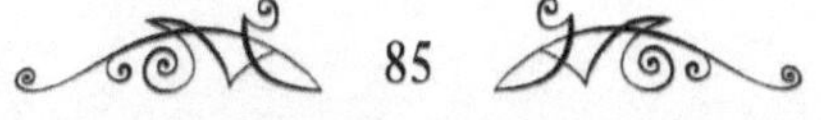

Wondering what that Dante man had been getting at. Wondering how every vampire here had been able to resist me, but Owen chose not to. Wondering too many hurtful things, so I dared not open my mouth for fear they would all burst out.

The stew was thick and sludgy, like a mix of veggies, porridge, and ground meat. There were no spices or salt to improve the flavor, but it went down easily enough and settled well in my empty stomach.

I had almost worked up the nerve to ask Owen some questions when the door opened again. Niamh and Lance had returned, and Joss and Ash came in after them.

It was time to meet the Synedrion.

7

KAITLYN

We marched down the long hallway in silence.

"That's it. I can't bear it anymore." I gave a melodramatic, exasperated sigh. "Which of you is Joss and which one is Ash?"

The ninja-like Ebonguard, one on either side of Owen and me, kept walking silently.

Then, "Joss," said the woman.

"Ash," said the man.

"Making friends with the Ebonguard now? I'm impressed. They aren't generally the friendly type. You're a special one indeed." Lance laughed, slowing to walk closer to us. The Ebonguard didn't seem to find it funny.

"Yeah, and maybe you monsters are too busy being monsters to care what each other's names are," I snapped.

Lance seemed almost hurt. "You might be right there. You know, it's Ebonguard tradition, during their initiation, to shed all but a single syllable for their name. And no, most don't speak to them. They are, even among us vampires, a bit intimidating." He shrugged, and picked up his pace again, moving ahead.

Me and my big mouth. I should have been trying to make friends here as much as possible. It was my only chance.

"Sorry," I muttered. "I'm a little out of sorts. Blame it on the blood loss. And being kidnapped. And held prisoner."

"Those things are likely to dampen your spirits." He slowed, returning to my side. "I'm sure things will be fine, but I wish there was something I could do to ease your concerns."

"You can," I said promptly. "You can hold off Joss and Ash—no offense guys, I know you're just doing your job—while Owen and I make a break for it. Easy peasy, done."

Joss and Ash didn't react to my open plotting at all. Talk about confidence in their role, or in how hopeless our escape attempt would be.

"Not so easy peasy. Firstly, I doubt I'd be physically able to hold off Joss and Ash. I'm not that powerful. Few vampires would be. Secondly, vampires are everywhere, and there is nowhere for the two of you to hide now."

"A very sunny part of the tropics sounds good to me. A small deserted island. I'm sure Owen could swing it. Or I'll sell the castle and trade up. On a side note, are you looking to buy a castle?"

"Aren't you charming?" Lance said. "Ready to make a real estate transaction out of a bad situation. I like that about you."

I had a feeling he liked my blood way more than my humor and charms. I also felt a really uncomfortable sensation set in at the words as I pondered the possibility that Lance was actually flirting with me. Right here. In front of Owen. Right after he'd almost killed me. The fucking nerve.

"What I like about *you* is that you're not drinking my blood. Let's keep it that way so I keep liking you. How about that?"

He put a wounded expression on his face, and played it up. "I already said I don't want any more of your blood. I will not hurt you again. Some of us can control our hungers."

We rounded a corner in the maze of corridors and were met with a mob of vampires blocking the way. We came to a stop.

"And some of us can't," Lance finished his thought.

"Clear the path," Niamh commanded.

One male vampire let out a low groan and I shrank

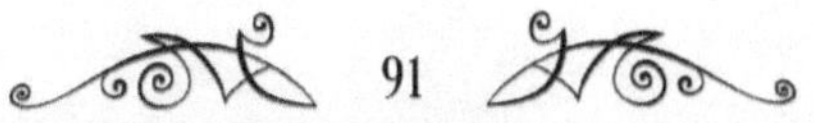

away, my arms tucking tightly to my sides. He jostled closer. "Soon, the council will decide they don't care for whatever you are, and stop protecting you. Then you'll be fair game. Then we'll all be drinking from you, taking turns, tasty thing."

Owen tensed, but before his slow human body could act, Lance stepped in front of me, shielding my body with his in an alpha male display of aggression. His stance screamed an ownership of me that neither I nor Owen appreciated, but the other vampires stepped back. Another warning from Niamh and the Ebonguard had them fleeing in a blur of speed.

Owen glared. He grunted, whispering in my ear, "He's acting like he's claimed you."

Lance heard this and turned to look Owen right in the eye. Like a challenge. Then he smiled. "Just a show. It will help keep her safe."

Owen clearly didn't like the idea either way. Neither did I.

I would not be some vampire's possession.

Before I could say anything, or maybe make a break out a window, a low ringing bell sounded. The bell, deep and timorous, made every vampire stiffen. Owen pulled me closer. His eyes looked into mine. "The council is waiting on us."

We followed Niamh through echoing hallways and past empty rooms. The place had a strange deserted feel despite the things living inside of it. A dry, bitter smell hung over everything.

We exited one corridor into a much wider and taller hallway. In the shadow beside me, a man stood, poised to attack. His fangs were bared, his arms outstretched.

I gasped and stumbled back into Owen. The man standing to the side of the hall made no other move. No move at all—nor would he ever, I saw. He was a statue made of charcoal-colored stone.

My heart still pounding, I saw more hideous statues lining each wall of the hallway. Owen steadied me as I looked around at them. Some were frozen mid-attack. Some cowered or begged. One appeared to be asleep. Some were women, some men. All were vampires, and all had an expression of agony on their faces.

What a way to welcome people into the council chambers. A nice little reminder of the consequences of possible verdicts, I supposed.

Owen squeezed my shoulder but offered no explanation. We moved down the strange gauntlet of horrifying statues.

We reached a set of double doors at the end of the hallway and Niamh opened them.

Lance, Owen and I went through; the others remained outside. As the door behind us closed I stopped in my tracks. My eyes went wide.

There was a raised dais that led up to a massive fall of limestone, like a waterfall made of melted bones.

Seven thrones were carved into the rock, each equal in size, and the falls were spotted with candlelight. Rivers of wax dripped from them, blending into the ivory limestone underneath. Tapestries in dark bloody colors hung from the other walls. Velvety red carpets covered the floor and steps leading to the thrones.

The ceiling was high, at least three stories, right to the top of the natural cavern. There were no windows. It was stifling, not only because the air was thick and heavy either, but because that color scheme, which should have been decadent and opulent, felt oppressive and too-heavy. It appeared to have been unchanged for centuries.

A herald of some kind was announcing our entrance and making long and tedious introductions and instructions in a droning thrall voice.

But my only thoughts were on the seven who sat on those thrones. I didn't want to look. I somehow knew, on a primitive and cellular level, that monsters sat there. Not just monsters, the rulers of monsters. No matter how much I told myself to keep my head down, my curiosity got the better of me. I looked up, then openly gawked at the seven vampires seated in the chairs that ranged along the raised dais.

Five were women. One had hair the color of flame. Her skin was so pale and so perfect, and her neck so long and slender, that she could have been a pre-Raphaelite portrait that had somehow had life breathed into it. Okay, maybe not life, an animated un-death. She wore a jade-colored gown made of a heavy brocade fabric, and an emerald and ruby necklace that encircled her neck like a high collar.

Owen saw me looking. "That is Delphine. Next to her is Shirina, Milton, Lin, Viatrix, Toren, and Bertha."

Putting names to the faces didn't help make them more human. Delphine had a regal, imperious demeanor, and as her eyes locked with mine, the corners of her mouth, lips as reddened as a ripe raspberry, lifted upward slightly.

I hastily looked away to the next in the row.

With hair that fell like a black waterfall all the way to the ground, and an elegantly curved nose, Shirina wore a tight royal-blue gown with a very low neckline that showed off her other elegant and abundant curves. Sapphires winked and flashed from her throat, her hands, and her ears.

The man next to her, as golden as she was dark, looked at me with black vampire eyes that were in stark contrast to his glowing god-like appearance. Milton's ivory blond hair, and a light, honey tan, were played up by an all-white suit. *How on earth does he have a tan?* It had to be a spray-on.

Lin seemed the most normal. Uncomfortably normal, like she could have stepped out of an office

meeting, with her neat, mousey brown hair, her pant-suit, and her smile that was both disingenuous and frightening.

Viatrix was the one furthest from normal. It was like there was no color at all in her skin or hair. She sat still, like part of the stone around her, her eyes closed, her ashy dress of dripping lace giving the impression she was crumbling to dust right in front of us.

The male vampire next to her, Toren, looked as I would imagine Merlin, or some other ancient wizard, to appear. His body was old, his skin crepey and translucent, his hair white, but he had no stiffness or stoop that came with age. He sat tall and alert, strong and clear.

I knew vampires could be any age, whatever age they were turned, and stay that way, but I'd always imagined them young. And Bertha was at the youngest end of the age spectrum, a teenager by appearance. I wondered if there were younger vampire children out there, or if turning children was taboo even for these monsters.

My mouth hung slightly agape as I studied Bertha. She appeared to be no older than eighteen, but her petite form was dressed in a way more suited to an adult. A white silk shirt in a modern cut was worn casually, collar loose, under a herringbone blazer. Her blond hair was trimmed short in a no-nonsense pixie-cut.

As I observed her, the teen vampire yawned widely, not bothering to cover it either.

The vampire with the flaming red hair spoke in a sharp tone, "Bertha, if you cannot concentrate on your duties, perhaps we should relieve you of them."

The herald, who had been continuing his droning announcements about the glory and honor of the original seven, halted, and his last words echoed throughout the chamber.

Bertha gave Delphine an insolent glare. "There's nothing wrong with my concentration, thank you. I just wish you would dispense with the boring ceremony and get on with it already. We're here to discuss Miss French, not bore her to death with pompous speeches." She looked over to me then. "Loved you in *The Way You Do*, by the way."

I opened my mouth to say thank you, but my voice had been stunned silent. That was the movie I'd had a role in right after being freed by Owen. I guess it shouldn't have been surprising that vampires watched movies too, but it just seemed such a human thing. I warmed up toward Bertha a little bit.

"I agree. About this meeting, I mean. Let's get to the matter at hand," Milton said, his smooth and debonair voice insinuating itself into the conversation. "We do have much to discuss, about some rather concerning developments."

Delphine sat rigid. Her lips twitched around her words. "We honor the original seven by continuing the traditions which they started. We hold their seats only until they return."

Bertha snorted. "They won't return. It is ridiculous to keep believing silly myths. We are in the twenty-first century! Yet you insist on continuing to embrace the past as if it were a lover you cling to, despite them having long since turned into bone and ash."

Silence filled the chamber. Behind me were rows upon rows of pew seating, all empty. Maybe these meetings normally had a crowd of spectators which hadn't been allowed in this time. I wondered if the council would talk to each other like this in front of a crowd of their peers rather than just our small group of two humans and a vampire who had a close call with humanity.

"This is the vampire made human then?" Lin said, her voice loud and firm, ignoring any pettiness around her.

Lance went forward a few steps and knelt before the seven. "It is. Owen Raine and I were old friends. I had been seeking him out. I saw him at the airport and was taken aback by the sight of him, because all I could sense and smell was human. Nothing but human, yet he looked like the one I once called friend."

He rose again, continuing, "I followed these two to their home, and confronted them. I was shocked to discover that it was true. Somehow, Owen had become human, but I was overcome by the desire for the woman's blood." Lance bowed his head. "After tasting her, feeling the effects of her blood, I made the connection and drew the confession from them, that she was the cause. As you can see that one feed has not managed to strip me of my immortality."

Toren nodded. "The doctor's report confirms it. Owen Raine is completely human. Lancelot Ferland did have a marginally higher core temperature than normal, but no other side effects."

"Physical side effects," Lance qualified. "I have also felt a change in my emotions since drinking from her. That is worth noting."

"Oh, interesting indeed," muttered Shirina. "Shall Raine remain human forever? Will he return to his vampire form? Does he crave blood even though he is human? Will he live longer, or will the years spent as a vampire accelerate his aging now he is a human? Does his blood now carry the affliction that would turn vampires human if drunk? There are too many variables. How are we to make a decision here until we have done more research on the subjects?"

"We can decide that it is clearly an abomination," spat Milton. "We must put it to death. Both of them. The once vampire and that ..." His dark eyes held nothing but disgust, "... *thing* that would bring so much strife and discord to our lives. Let's be done

with this nonsense."

I tried to speak up for myself, but Lin's firm, business-like voice beat me. "Somehow, as much as we tried to keep this quiet, news of the changed one spread before they had even arrived in Umbravallis." All eyes in the room turned briefly to Lance before Lin continued, "Our vampire kin know this is now a possibility, and some may even want it for themselves. If we simply dispose of this potential cure without even considering its uses, there will be a lot of anger."

"Cure?" Milton tensed on his throne, as if he were about to jump out of it and right at me. "We have nothing that needs to be cured. We are perfection immortal. Choosing to become a weak, finite human again is like choosing euthanasia."

"Which some would argue is a valid choice," Lin returned.

"And some would argue it is not," Milton spat back.

Wow, I thought. Politics were politics whether you were dealing with humans or vampires, it seemed.

Delphine, who had been seething silently as her companions had their free-for-all debate, finally spoke again, "Tell me, human, how do you do it?"

I swallowed, my mouth suddenly dry, knowing now was the time to try to talk my way out of this, and knowing I was not the person for the job. My mouth generally talked me into trouble, not out of it. "My name is Kaitlyn, Kaitlyn French," I offered, trying to buy time. "And I have no idea how I do it. I'd say we know it's something about my blood. Drink it, and it makes you more human. Drink enough, you're human for good. That's what happened to Owen, and started for Lance. But I'm not really working with a large sample size."

Crap. Did I just give them a reason to start drinking from me to test the theory? Realizing that, I added, very quickly, "What I mean is, we don't know enough, and I honestly couldn't say what would happen to any other vampires if you tried it. If I have some kind of weird vampirism-killing virus in me, it could affect different vampires in different ways, like a bad allergic reaction or something." I let out a *whew* under my breath, hoping I'd said the right thing.

Lin eyed me for a moment, and with a small, sly smile, said, "It's a correct enough assumption without any further evidence. We could die from that blood. Not only because it could potentially turn us human, and humans are weak and frail and die, but just from the act of drinking it."

"All the more reason to put it to death. It's a danger to us," Milton said. "Its very presence disgusts me."

Fury sizzled and spiked along my spine.

Oblivious to my emotions, Toren asked, "How many times did you drink from her, Owen?"

Owen shook his head. Shame coated his face. "More times than I would like to admit. I could feel the change, but never understood the final consequences of my actions. I kept her and drank from her for weeks."

My heart felt heavy at the memory, but I reached my hand out to his and held it, offering again my silent forgiveness.

Bertha eyed our hands with an intense expression. "Just look at his human sadness, at their joined hands. I do so miss that connection of empathy. As much as I struggled to hold onto the memory of how it felt, it is all gone from me. If we decide that they may live but are too dangerous out in the world, I would keep them as my pets to be voyeur to such feelings."

Did she just put dibs on us? I stared, speechless. Any warmth I might have felt to Bertha before was gone.

"You may find she's already been claimed," Delphine murmured with a sly smile.

A deep frown marred Owen's face as his gaze traveled between Lance and me. His lips thinned, and I could see that he was still angry enough to kill if he had to. The idea chilled me, that even now as a human, to kill seemed like a natural response for him.

Lin said, "Could it be genetic? We'll have to test other members of her family."

"What?" My thoughts flashed to my poor, simple, country mom and dad. "No, this doesn't have anything to do with anyone in my family. I mean, wouldn't you have known? Wouldn't this have surely happened some time before in history if there was a whole family tree out there of irresistible blood that turned vampires human?"

"Not if a single feed isn't enough to bring the change. Not if the vampire couldn't control themselves and killed during the first feeding. Have you ever had family members disappear before?" Toren asked.

"No. My family is as boring as boring can be—no missing bodies, no scandals, no vampires. I'd like it to stay that way."

I didn't get a reassurance there either way. They didn't seem to care for my opinions or negotiations at all. I had no leverage.

Lin looked to Shirina. "Oh, I can't wait to get some samples into the lab."

Shirina nodded enthusiastically.

Guess my lab-rat fears were founded.

Shirina tossed her shimmering black hair. "I, for one, can't wait to drink from the cup of her neck. That blood smells so sweet. Whatever price is involved it will be worth paying. I crave a taste. There's something so tempting about her smell, like fresh, ripe berries. It has been so long since I've had a berry in my mouth. I have to taste her, at least once."

My limbs froze. And there I thought she was the logical one.

Toren gave me a long, assessing look. "I would suggest that none drink from her until we know more, even though she smells so delicious."

"Or from Owen," Lance cut in. His expression had become drawn, and his already pale skin seemed nearly white. "His blood was made human by hers, and who could know what effects it may have?"

Delphine's hand lifted and silence fell. Her eyes locked onto mine yet again, and I thought I saw that smile lift her mouth once more. Yet she was not smiling at all when she spoke, "We will now vote on this matter. You have been brought here because your deaths have been called for. Regardless of what your blood can do, we are to decide if you live or die. The Synedrion shall vote now."

That was it? We didn't get to make our case or anything? We didn't have any say?

Shirina said, "I vote they live. What this human has done is not a crime."

Milton's vote was obvious. "I vote for death. She has, in essence, killed a vampire. Our laws are strict about such matters."

Toren waved a hand. "Our law only calls for death for vampires who have killed other vampires."

"And for humans who dare hunt us," Milton snarled. "They carried Nemexia."

Delphine glowered, a sparkle in her dark eyes.

Toren shrugged. "Troubling, but not a crime

for a human. It's been confiscated, and there's no evidence it was used on a vampire. The woman didn't hunt Raine, nor has she yet killed him. Our law says nothing of humans who inadvertently cause an inevitable death to a vampire through a return to mortality."

Delphine spoke again, "We vote. Those against death, raise your hand."

My heart literally shook in my chest as I surveyed the hands lifted for keeping us alive. Lin, Shirina, and Toren. Only three of the seven. We were dead.

Delphine said, "Those for death."

Surprise, surprise, Milton's hand was the first one in the air. Then Delphine's. Then Viatrix, who'd remained with her eyes closed and so still I thought she may have been asleep through the whole meeting.

Delphine surveyed her companions with a look of distaste. "You abstain, Bertha?"

Bertha's forehead creased in a frown. "We do not know that she is dangerous. But we do not know that she is not. It may be that some vampires wish to become human, and if they had that wish they should have the antidote within her blood. It should be a choice. So many of us weren't given a choice. We were turned wholly against our will." She looked down at me, head tilted ever so slightly. "On the other hand, her blood could be a weapon. It could be used to decimate our ranks. If our enemies came

into possession of her blood, they could use it against us, steal away our power with it, to the point where they could exterminate us entirely."

Silence settled on us like a blanket. It lay heaviest on me, its weight crushing. Bertha was right. When she put it like that, my blood could be a huge threat to their whole kind. To their ways, to their continuation as a species. I wasn't sure if that was a good or bad thing, but it was a dangerous thing, for me.

"We have three who wish for death, three who do not, and one who has abstained." Delphine sighed. "We do not have a majority. Until we can break the tie, nothing shall be done with them. We must consider all the things that Bertha has mentioned, as well as many others. We must spend more time to truly consider all the points that we should before we make our decision. We will deliberate, and return."

Sweat broke out along my hairline at the uncertain verdict. We would live, but for how long?

8

OWEN

The Ebonguard met us outside the Synedrion's chambers, and we were escorted back to the palatial suite that we had been in before. Kaitlyn tried to make small talk with our guards, to no response, on the way. I could see the nervous energy filling her and felt the same myself.

When the heavy door shut us in and locked, she stared up at me. Tears sprang into her eyes. I watched her fight them back.

"You were quiet back there," she said.

My jaw twitched. "I was so angry. If I'd spoken, it would have been to threaten their deaths, and that wouldn't have helped us at all. But I would burn them in their beds if they touched you."

I reached for her hands and she shied away from

me, so my fingers wrapped in on themselves instead, making fists. If I were only still a vampire, I would have the strength to break down these walls, and how I felt now, I was almost ready to try, vampire strength or no.

No natural light reached the windows of our room with the palace too far in the back of the cave, in the deep, shadowed valley, but it must have been near morning. I was exhausted, and Kaitlyn's eyes were rimmed red with gray smudges beneath.

She turned her face from mine before I could kiss her tiredness away.

"What is that smell?" she said.

An appetizing aroma met my nostrils, and I stepped back, my head turning as I tried to figure out where it was coming from.

A table had been set with the finest china, heavy and well-polished silver, crisp white linen, and heavy crystal. A far nicer spread than had been provided before.

Kaitlyn almost skipped over. Her unending, joyous curiosity for food always pleased me. But a lump formed in my throat. I wondered what this meal had been left here for, why we were being given more than the gruel afforded the thralls. Was this meant to be our last meal?

I said nothing to Kaitlyn though. She deserved something to take her mind off our situation.

I pulled a chair out for her in a courtly, gentlemanly gesture.

We lifted the lids to find a stunning array of fresh fruits, and no less than six different varieties of cheese in generous serves. Crackers and sweet biscuits were also arranged around the fruit and cheese on the tray.

The door opened as Kaitlyn took her first bite, and Lance entered.

"Not only are we imprisoned, we also have no freedom as to who enters our chambers and when," I muttered.

Kaitlyn tsked at me and whispered back, "He's trying to be a friend."

And we needed all the friends we could get right now. I knew that too. But I didn't know how long I could stay friends with some*thing* who looked at Kaitlyn the way Lance did.

Along with him, one of the Ebonguard entered to stand guard on the inside of our room. Apparently, even Lance wasn't trusted to be alone with us.

Lance pulled up a seat at our table. He smiled, but lines around his eyes and eyebrows gave away his concern. "Please, don't let me interrupt you. In fact, I was hoping to enjoy watching you eat."

Kaitlyn's nose wrinkled with embarrassment in a way that was far too adorable.

She kept eating, although less at ease than when

she'd begun. My appetite was gone, replaced by a seething hatred like lava inside me.

"So, old friend," I said, "how do you see our chances now?"

Lance had been watching Kaitlyn lick the juice of a pear off her fingers, but turned away and sighed. "Yes, I was wrong. I truly didn't expect such hostility against you. I wish I'd made a different choice yesterday, but I was so distraught over what Kaitlyn's blood had done to me that I didn't think. I contacted the Synedrion because I couldn't contain the immensity of what had happened within myself. I should have said nothing, and let you go. I'm sorry."

Before I could reply, Kaitlyn said, "We might be more willing to accept your apology if it came with the keycode to this room, and a key to a fast car."

"Or return our perfume of Nemexia to us," I grumbled.

"You know that's illegal for a vampire to possess. If I had taken it from your luggage myself, I would be just as imprisoned as you and no help. What you had is probably destroyed. I will help you as much as I can, but it is not simple. Now that they know of the two of you, they will track you and they will hunt you anywhere you go. Ebonguard put your human Mounties to shame in that regard. And if you escape from here, it will make their verdict decided and they *will* kill you. Stay. Be patient. You do stand a chance. The Synedrion deliberates, and you have powerful allies upon it."

He was right. I tried to calm the anger in me. It was hard. I didn't remember if it had been this hard to control my emotions when I was human before, or if I was struggling because I had had to relearn it all again within a few months. "I understand, Lance. I, too, was torn and confused at the taste of her blood. I, too, suffered from the sudden onset of things I hadn't experienced in a great many years. I had what I could only refer to as terrible mood swings."

Kaitlyn nodded vehemently in agreement as she chewed.

Lance said, "If there was a way to release you, I would. They don't trust me now either, and while I'm free to move around, I doubt I'm free to leave this place. They have declared me to be something … in between. Not human, but not vampire either. I have no idea what I am now." There was a very real sorrow in his voice.

"I'm sorry," Kaitlyn said.

I slammed my fist on the table in a way that rattled the cutlery. "Don't be sorry! It's not your fault. How could it be? He chose to drink your blood, and you had no say in the matter. You tried to warn him not to. You tried to fight him away. Don't give him your sympathy for the consequences of his actions."

Kaitlyn frowned at me, frozen. She blinked, then said to Lance, "Maybe, as long as you don't drink

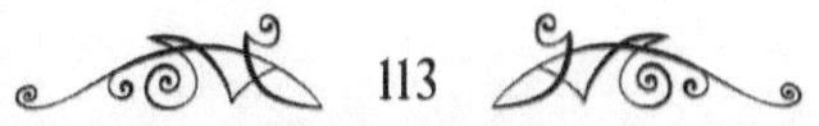

anymore of my blood, you will go back to being the same old vampire you were before. Until you change completely, I doubt it's permanent."

Lance's fingers twisted around each other. "I don't know that I want to go back to being what I was before."

I growled in a low whisper, "You may not drink more from her, Lance."

Lance recoiled. "How many times do I have to tell you that I don't wish to? The last thing on Earth I want to be is human. I've come to accept and appreciate my immortality. Even after all these centuries, the idea of a final death is a terror I don't want to face. But I don't mind the sensation of these emotions that have resurfaced in me. I feel I have been reminded of who I used to be, who I wanted to be. A little bit of guilt can be a good thing."

A long, awkward silence fell around the table. Even Kaitlyn had stopped eating.

I stared down at my fists, and worked to release and stretch my fingers. Why could I not contain this anger in me? Was this who I was? Had I always been this hotheaded? The last few months with Kaitlyn had been so blissful, despite worries at the back of my mind. I hadn't been under any stress close to this level. I barely knew how to start dealing with it.

A man cleared his throat at the door. "He may not want your blood, but I do. Under the Synedrion's orders, of course."

Lance looked over his shoulder. "Ewan. Lin and Shirina worried these two won't last long enough to get their precious blood samples to the lab?"

The same doctor who had seen to us before walked in, set his bag right down next to our food, and began prepping sample tubes. "You know how they love some interesting blood samples."

Lance grinned wryly.

"I don't suppose I have any say in this?" Kaitlyn said, her hand wrapped around her inner elbow as though anticipating the needle.

I glared at Lance, hoping he would intervene. Neither Kaitlyn nor I had the strength to match a vampire. I didn't want this. However small the sample of blood, it was a theft, an intrusion, an abuse against my Strawberry.

"Neither of you do. I'm to get samples from both the ... humans." Ewan drawled the last word, looking me up and down with curious disgust.

I slammed my arm down on the table, offering myself first. The doctor moved quickly, drawing three vials, before strapping Kaitlyn's arm and drawing two from her.

He tapped her veins at her wrist and gave her skin a soft pinch. "That's all from you. Still need to replenish. I told you to hydrate."

And with that, he clipped his bag closed and

walked out.

Kaitlyn cleared her throat softly and asked, "You said that we had some allies? You weren't counting Lin and Shirina, were you?"

Lance smiled in an embarrassed sort of way. "At least their scientific interest in you is enough that I believe they would protect you at all costs. There are many against you, however. To some, this is a matter of the greater good, and they don't have the ability to care about you and your needs if they wanted to. They fear, and rightfully so, that our enemies may capture you and use you as a weapon against us."

"What enemies could vampires have?" she asked.

I offered her an answer, trying to let the facts clear my emotions. "The Synedrion lead the largest group of vampires, but there are others, those with different leaders and different values. Extremist groups, vying for a greater share of power and more influence."

"Enemies to all of us," Lance added. "Then there are those who would see themselves as human again. Who would accept that gift willingly. They will fight for your lives, but only if it benefits them."

Kaitlyn lifted her hands as though weighing the options. "And here we are, between extremists who want us eradicated from the world, and those who want to keep us and our special blood in their labs."

"Where do you stand, Lance?" I asked.

Lance's head lowered. "I stand with you, Owen. You were like my brother once, and I feel that bond again anew. And I stand with Kaitlyn, not only because I know that you love her. There are plenty of reasons to love her—even I can see that."

Kaitlyn blushed.

Just as I start to feel for Lance again, he says something like that, right in front of me.

I hid my anger under a smile. "Ignore his attempts, Kaitlyn. He always was a flirt. It seems some things don't change."

"I recall it was you who decided it was a good idea to tell women that I really was Lancelot of Arthur's court, an immortal knight come to woo them. Quite the wingman, you were."

I paused, my mouth open. I had forgotten that. When our friendship had ended, I left him behind and blocked out the memories of our good times together. He'd been there for me, helped me, from my darkest moments after Adelle died, when I almost became as bad as her. That was when he found me, taught me his ways. Taught me a vampire could be more than their urges, that even without empathy we could make the right choices.

Kaitlyn was looking between us. "I have literally a million questions."

Lance chuckled. "She says, hyperbolically."

My smile became sincere. Maybe I did still hold

some love for my friend. "How long until they come up with an answer?"

"They are likely going to rest now, so we know you have at least the day."

"A day." Kaitlyn almost sobbed the word. Her head shook, dark hair shimmering in waves around her. "What if we did escape? Really. There must be a way we could go underground, just … just …"

I said, "Kaitlyn, no. You deserve the life you have worked so hard to have. Even if we could live in hiding, I wouldn't ask you to live your life that way."

"Any life is better than no life at all!" she gasped.

I felt the same. But I had to keep up the appearance that we had some hope. What else could I do? I had some ideas, but we would have to be patient.

I stood from my chair and kneeled beside hers, wrapping my arms around her. She was shaking. She leaned into me.

Lance stood abruptly, the legs of his chair scraping across the floor with a loud racket. "I, too, must rest. I have no answers to the when and how the Synedrion will decide your fate. I shall endeavor, however, to send a thrall out to fetch you more food."

"You got this for us?" Kaitlyn asked.

"I arranged it to be delivered while you met with the Synedrion. There is no more food here other than the poor stuff they feed the thralls. I wanted to prove that vampires could be reasonable, even hospitable." Lance shook his head softly. "Even if the others proved me wrong, I shall continue to make sure that your stay is as comfortable as possible."

I could hear the sound of him walking away, the door scraping open and closed again, and then we were alone.

"We should rest, too," I said.

Kaitlyn nodded weakly, no doubt as physically and emotionally drained as I was. I bundled her up in my arms and lifted her from the chair. I carried her through to the adjoining bedroom and put her on her feet. We removed each other's clothes slowly, lovingly, and climbed beneath the sheets. She curled into my body and I wrapped myself around her like a shield, listening to her heart and mine, beating together.

Our precious lives.

I wouldn't let anything end those lives yet, not yet, not when we had spent so little time together.

I would kill anyone and anything that tried. I may not have been a vampire anymore, but I still had a way. A way I could remove anyone or anything that threatened us.

I still had the ring.

9

KAITLYN

I woke up feeling dehydrated and aching all over. The stresses and injuries of the previous days were taking their toll. Owen lay beside me, his bare chest rising and falling with the slow breath of sleep. He seemed so calm now, so peaceful. It was hard to remember the rage I'd seen in him not long ago.

I wasn't sure how I felt about him right then. He had such anger, such darkness in him. He reminded me too much of the monster I thought he'd left behind when he became human again. Had I been so naïve as to think those violent emotions were all gone now? Humans were capable of that much and more. Maybe I didn't know Owen, vampire or human, as well as I'd thought.

I slipped out of bed and stretched my body. A

grandfather clock read five o'clock, but I had no idea if that was AM or PM, or what time vampires kept in their cloistered little land here. International travel, vampire schedules, long sleeps, and long meetings had screwed with my body clock, and I couldn't place a bet if it were day or night.

I unzipped my luggage, wincing at the loud sound, worried it would wake Owen. I pulled out some clean underwear and a simple fuchsia-colored slip dress. The palace was cool, but not uncomfortably cold, either naturally because of the cave, or kept at a living temperature for the sake of the thralls and other humans on-site maybe. Certainly the vampires themselves didn't need it.

I had just pulled the dress over my head when Owen curled his arms around me from behind, smothering my neck with gentle kisses.

I held his arms back, and warmth filled me. With him I felt safe. I felt at home. Of course he'd been angry. I was angry too, at the unfairness of all of this.

I turned to face him and pressed my head to his chest. "They're not going to let us live, are they?"

"Someone once told me I should hope for the best but expect the worst. I suppose that's what I'm doing."

"They hate me so much," I whispered. What they thought about me shouldn't matter in the scheme of things, but it did. "Even the ones who want to keep me alive so they can find their own humanity again. I bet they despise the fact the cure came from a human, rather than one of their own."

"We have to play along until we can find a way to escape."

I nodded. "We have to get the F out of H."

I held Owen's hand as I turned to look around the room. I pointed to the windows. "We could shred the sheets, make a rope ladder. Break one of these windows and climb down."

It all sounded a bit fantastical, but the act of laying out a plan, even a crazy one, lifted my spirits. "There are probably still cars out the front. We grab one with a thrall driver so we can get the keys. We can't take out a vamp, but we could get past a thrall. We do it when the vamps are sleeping."

Owen had a very small smile on his face, but it faded almost as soon as it appeared. "Ebonguard never sleep. They are probably listening to this conversation right now, and would be upon us the moment the window broke."

"Only one way to test that theory," I offered, hopefully.

Owen shook his head. "Where do we go after that? It's a long drive out of Umbravallis, and some vampires can travel on foot as fast as a car can drive. Neither of us know how to fly a helicopter or plane, if we could even hijack one. If we could get back to Slovakia … there is something in the castle

that could help us, but only against a single enemy at a time, not against the hoard of vampires that might come after us."

My curiosity and hope spiked. "What could help us?"

Owen's eyebrows lowered, and he looked down. "It would be the first place they would look for us though. We can't go back there. Not yet."

I wanted to ask again what it was, but his glower made me stay quiet.

"We just have to hold out a bit longer. We have to cherish every moment we still have," he said, and pulled my chest into his, pressing his lips to mine.

Just like that, my temperature spiked about five degrees. It seemed impossible, maybe even a little wrong somehow for me to be so turned on, for me to want him so badly when our lives were in so much danger.

Perhaps that was exactly why it was so right. We had no idea if this was to be our last day on Earth. If it was, I didn't want to regret not knowing his body against mine, the feel of his lips on mine, and the touch of his skin against mine, one last time before I died.

I slid my hands down the rippled muscles of his bare back until they reached the silky satin of his boxers. Owen's mouth found my neck, laying down a trail of kisses. Even as a human, he was still very much a neck guy.

Remortality

Time coalesced to the distance between heartbeats and nothing more or less. My breath caught in my throat and my fingers wound into his hair. Our mouths met again in a wild and passionate kiss that said everything we could have ever tried to say to each other in our final moments—words of love, and desire, and hope, and despair, all of it written by our tongues. The things left undone and unsaid that may never get the chance to be spoken, or put into action, all the things we had hoped for, and still hoped for, even as we knew they may never be.

My legs wrapped tight around his waist, and I let my hands move from his hair to his shoulders, relishing the strength in his muscles. His breath washed over my neck and cheek as he spoke, and I shivered. It was still hot when he called me Strawberry, even if his reasons for it had changed.

A loud thump came from the living room of our quarters, freezing us in place.

Owen gently let me go and crept to the door. He held his hand out to warn me back, but I had to peek out too.

One of our Ebonguard lay motionless on the carpet inside the entrance door.

Our second Ebonguard was being dragged inside by Delphine. She dropped them to the ground with a second matching thump before clicking the door closed behind her.

"What the actual fuck?" I whispered.

Her black eyes glared at me. Her mouth turned to the same small smile she'd given me in the meeting.

Horror threatened to topple me toward the floor.

She moved toward us, her body swaying elegantly. "It is time to die, humans."

I shook my head. It didn't make sense. If the council had come to a decision, why had she turned our guards into ragdolls?

Owen must have had the same thought. "Taking matters into your own claws, Delphine? The Synedrion hasn't yet ordered our deaths. You will be stripped from your position and worse if you touch us."

"Yeah," I shot over Owen's broad shoulder. "I thought you were all about tradition. You can't kill us until you've got your damned majority."

"By killing you both I am saving tradition. What if what you have is a virus, spread through contact rather than blood? You have to be destroyed, now. What I do will save all vampires. I would take the risk for that." Delphine traced a finger down the side of her face, brushing back her flame-red hair. "But no one will know it was me. I used a thrall to scent your guards with Nemexia—thanks for bringing some with you, by the way. Now your guards will awaken to find you dead with no evidence of who killed you. They will likely take the blame themselves, if, say, there were someone on the council who could push that motion." Her grin was terrifying.

She stalked closer. The aquamarine couture gown she wore was at odds with her menacing prowl. I thought she could have dressed a bit more appropriately for murder, but if this was what she normally wore, it might have aroused suspicion if she started wandering the halls in black-ops gear.

She didn't rush. Her slow confidence held every threat of the truth of how powerful she was compared to us.

She seemed surprised when Owen picked up a chair and swung it at her. The chair hit hard enough to knock her off balance, but not enough to fell her. The chair splintered into pieces, and I grabbed a large and wickedly jagged chunk.

I didn't hesitate. I lunged straight for Delphine's heart.

She twisted her torso away and swiped her clawed hand at me.

I inhaled sharply as I ducked under her attack, jabbing out with my other fist. My agent had set me up with hand-to-hand combat training, hoping to score me some lucrative action movie parts. I sent a silent thank you across the world to him.

I landed that punch in Delphine's lower stomach, but it felt like punching a concrete wall covered in silk.

Obviously unharmed, she swatted me with one quick flick of her arm, and knocked me completely

back across the room and into a wall. The stake flew from my grasp.

My back hit the wall so hard that all the breath escaped from my lungs, flying out of my mouth with a loud squeaking sound.

Owen snatched the chunk of wood from where it had landed. He stalked Delphine around the room. Her hand casually swept furniture aside, blocking Owen's path to her. Her smile remained. This was a game for her. She would kill us in a flash when she was ready.

Owen jabbed the stake at Delphine and came very close to impaling her. Not close enough, however.

Run, get help, I begged Owen silently, because I didn't have enough air in my lungs yet to speak, or follow those instructions myself.

Owen flipped the stake around and used it like a baseball bat, hitting Delphine so hard that the wood splintered again and left Owen holding two smaller stakes.

I looked to our Ebonguard, lying lifeless on the ground not far from me. I wished they would wake up. I had no idea how long the Nemexia stuff would last. I felt a strange sort of betrayal that they hadn't protected us.

My elbows, and then my hands, found the wall, and I worked my way up it into a standing position. I ran to the door and tugged at the handle. Locked.

I hammered at the door. Surely someone would hear the commotion, notice our missing guards. Would no one help us?

I turned back to the fray.

A scream of fury ripped from my mouth as one of Delphine's hands came out and her claw-like fingernails left bloodied furrows along Owen's right cheek.

It was as though my scream shattered every window in the room. Glass exploded around us, and hooded figures poured in, too many of them to count.

Has help arrived at last? Are we saved?

Delphine hesitated, but Owen ignored the chaos, taking his chance to lunge with a small stake in each hand. Before he could drive them home, Delphine's attention snapped back and she knocked his arms aside with one hand and pushed him away with the other. Owen landed on an overturned lounge, then rolled to one side, landing on his feet with the stakes still held in both fists. I ran to his side.

Delphine looked at the figures in the room, advancing on her, their tattered brown robes swishing around them like whispers of death. She roared at them.

An all-encompassing terror overwrote everything else that I felt. The figures overwhelmed Delphine. One lifted her into the air, then with a casual, effortless

motion, ripped her head right off her shoulders.

Blood, a disgusting fountain of it, spouted from the stump of her neck, dark and thick. Her arms and legs twitched in a grotesque parody of a dance, and the scent of decay filled the room. Blood splashed across the ceiling and then rained back down, falling onto the floorboards and the broken and scattered furniture.

My mind went completely, utterly blank. I simply couldn't process what I had seen. It was too horrific. It was so horrific that there was no way it could be real, only it was.

The hooded figures came toward us. I shrank back, tears running down my face. I had hoped that the enemy of my enemy must have been my friend, but they proved that was a lie within seconds.

These new creatures were not our saviors.

Two of them grabbed me. I screamed, but a rough, dry hand covered my mouth. Wild-eyed, I looked for their faces to identify our new attackers, but every one of them was covered in a leathery mask shadowed by a heavy hood.

More of the robed figures grabbed at Owen. He fought hard, managing to stake one of them. I didn't know what it was that Owen had killed, but it wasn't human. A yellow-brown dust rose from the staked corpse as it crumbled away, smelling like mold and something else, something gruesome and *dry*.

Remortality

Five more of the hooded figures were on Owen. He disappeared beneath a pile of flapping robes and leather masks that covered the entire heads and faces of the new arrivals. I could hear his anguished cries until a final crack sounded that destroyed my heart, and he was quiet.

I whipped my face free of the muffling hand on me. I screamed so long and so loud that it tore up my vocal cords.

Something hit me in my temple.

Darkness swam in and took me down.

10

KAITLYN

I awoke to the sight of crumbling cave walls moving past me. My vision was blurry, and a thick pain gouged into my belly, making it hard for me to breathe. I blinked a few times, trying to figure out what was happening.

I was bent over the shoulder of one of the robed vampires. He moved fast. My head banged against his lower back. I smelled a disgusting *wormy* smell on the brown robes that flapped around the creature's body.

Vomit rose in my throat. The ache in my temple intensified, making my head spin. My fists raised and I brought them down onto a body that felt like gnarled wood.

My screams echoed down the hallway. I heard Owen's voice, coming from somewhere ahead of me.

It lifted into curses and promises to kill every single vampire that had taken us hostage. I could hear the sound of his fists striking against the cold flesh of the creature who carried him through the dim tunnel. We went deeper. Goosebumps rose on my skin as the temperature dropped. Mucky, musty air filled my lungs.

Were we still in Umbravallis? In the cave of the Synedrion palace? Or some other cave in some other place entirely? Only an occasional sconce with burning oil lit the way.

Soon, the crumbling dirt walls changed to bricks of stone, creating neat hallways which branched out along the way.

The air got thicker and even harder to breathe, the claustrophobic sensation taking me right to the edge of full-blown panic.

Owen's voice, raised in yet another curse, and the sound of a vampire hissing in pain, brought me back from that abyss. He was still here, somewhere, with me. I shuddered all over but was ready to keep fighting again.

I wrenched my body around, kicking off the vampire who had me over his shoulder. I fell away from him, right into another. Hands grabbed at me in the darkness and I hit them away.

My skin tightened into goosebumps and tears filled my eyes, but I kept fighting, no matter how repulsed by their touch and terrified of them I was.

Remortality

I had to fight back, had to. No matter how uneven the odds, I intended to fight for my life.

My life.

The life I had almost had right there in my fingertips. The career that had just started. The roles that might have followed.

I fought for Owen.

Owen and all that we could have had.

Tears ran down my face as I managed to claw my fingers under one vampire's leather mask and yanked it away. It satisfied me, as though I'd ripped its very skin from its face.

The sound of seams tearing was loud, but it vanished beneath my screams as I finally saw the face below the hood.

My heart stopped for a full second. I choked on hysteria as every horror movie I had ever seen, as the terror of that LARP game that had landed me with Owen, as the memory of having woken up hanging on the wall like a trapped butterfly, as every vision of every twisted creature of darkness all came rushing in at me, threatening to snap my very sanity.

I was shoved back and landed on a cold, slippery floor that stank so badly I heaved.

Just enough light showed the bars of the cell locking me in, and the face I'd torn the mask off.

Another scream ripped from my mouth and my sanity fled into the dark.

11

KAITLYN

"Wake up. Wake up, Kaitlyn. Strawberry, Strawberry, answer me. Wake up."

The words drifted in and out of my mind. My eyes opened and closed.

Sickness hit at the same time the smell did. I rolled over and retched pitifully, thanking my stars that there was nothing in my stomach to add to the stench. I may have complained that a prison was a prison while being kept in palatial comfort, but now I understood that everything was relative. This wasn't just a prison. This really was a dank, dirty dungeon.

Owen's voice reached me again. "I hear you. It's okay, it is. I love you. I love you, and I'm so sorry." I heard the slam of flesh against metal. Owen growled,

"If I were still a vampire, I could break these bars and save you right now."

I made it to my feet. My hands felt gross, and I wiped them on my filthy and bedraggled dress. Owen's cell must have been next to mine, but we were separated by a stone wall. I went to the bars and turned my head, hoping to see him. His hand came out and I extended mine. Our fingers could touch, only slightly, but that touch reassured me.

"Owen, don't. Don't do that to yourself. If you were still a vampire, there'd be no need to try to save me because I'd already be dead. We would never have been together if you were still a vampire. So don't. Don't do that. The only things to blame are ..."

The memory of the face I had seen when I yanked that mask off came flooding back to me. That horror, seared into my brain.

A shriveled face, so shriveled that the outlines of jawbone and eye sockets had been visible under the yellow-gray leathery flesh. Wrinkled lips were sewn shut with thick thread, the ragged stitches so clumsy and large they looked childish. Bulging black eyeballs surrounded by gray pouches of flesh sagged toward the sunken, dark hollows that once were cheeks.

My voice quavered, "What are they?"

"The Starved."

I gulped. "Say what?"

"The Starved. A cult of vampires that don't feed. They sew their lips shut so they can't. Not that some haven't. At times, the hunger gets to the ones who pledge themselves and they have ripped out the stitches in order to drink."

"Oh." I closed my eyes, trying not to imagine that. "Why don't they feed? Do they think it's wrong?"

"No, they don't value life. They think humans are filthy animals, that their blood taints their purity."

The words I had hoped to hear were, 'they sure do think it's wrong,' and, 'no worries they are our friends!'

I managed to drag a long breath into my lungs. "We've been kidnapped by a cult of perpetually hangry vampires?"

The small grasp Owen's fingers had on mine tightened. His voice echoed off the stone walls. "Damn Delphine. If she hadn't scented our Ebonguard, they could have protected us from this. And damn me for providing her with the Nemexia."

"What exactly is it, this Nemexia stuff?"

"Perfume of a rare corpse flower. The scent renders a vampire unconscious."

"Nemexia, wormwood, what else? What other weapons are there? What else don't I know? You should've told me these things, all of them. I should've known and been able to defend myself. At least known to wear that perfume you gave me every damn day!"

I grew frantic, hating that I took it out on him, but needing to vent all the same.

Owen was quiet for a moment. No other sound reached us, only a heavy, foreboding silence. "There's a lot about vampires you don't know. I simply haven't had the time to tell you everything. But I also purposefully hid things that I could have shared. You deserved to know. I should have told you more."

I felt his fingers slipping away from mine and pulled them back. "I get it, okay? You thought you could keep it all from me. That we could just be regular, oblivious humans together. But here we are. Just promise me the truth now. All of it. I need to know everything."

Two deep breaths of silence passed, then, "I promise."

"Okay then. The Starved, how do they stay alive if they don't drink blood?"

"I don't know. It's said they don't drink human, animal, or vampire blood. They take nothing. It's dangerous to go too long without; it destroys the body and the mind."

Insane vampires. I let that thought settle into my stomach like cement.

"No one knows exactly how long the Starved have abstained. Some break and drink before fasting again. Some shrivel away to nothing and die. But there are rumors some haven't fed in decades."

"It destroys their bodies? Does that mean they're

weak?"

"Weaker than a vampire who feeds? Yes. Weaker than us? No."

That didn't sound so good. I shifted, trying to reach farther, but there was no way.

The corridor outside my cell was empty and dark. My thoughts were equally bleak and dim. "What happens to us now? I take it they aren't exactly our friends."

"No, they aren't. I don't know what they would want with us."

"They probably won't want to eat us though. So, there's that."

Owen coughed a small, desperate laugh that quickly faded.

The silence spread out. I looked around, my eyes blurring with fatigue and hunger. There was so much pain in my heart. Tears leaked and dripped off my chin, but I made no sound. I had to be strong, and not just for me.

"When we get out of this, I want you to know, I'm okay with doing whatever we have to do to survive." The words wrenched their way from my throat. "Being an actress, having roles in movies, being in the public eye—I have to accept that is incompatible with who I am, what my blood can do."

"Don't lose hope for being who you want to be," Owen whispered, but despite his words, his conviction

sounded weak. He knew it was true, too.

My destiny had been tied to the vampire world from the moment Owen tasted my blood. Here I was now, wondering how I'd even survive the next day, let alone what my life would mean if I could keep that life, but not the dreams and desires that made it worth living.

Owen's fingers moved, brushing against mine in a soothing gesture. And him. Could I stay with him, the one who had brought me into all of this? Would I continue to love him if we had to live on the run, as the resentment of my crushed dreams built in me? Could I be happy to be alive and with him as my one love, giving up all else?

I shivered, not from the cold, but because deep inside I didn't have an answer. I didn't want to choose. I wanted him, I wanted our love, I wanted my career, and I wanted our lives. Why couldn't I have it all? It wasn't fair. I was strong. I'd been through so much. I was ...

"I'm valuable," I said, stunned by the revelation.

"Of course you are," Owen replied.

"No, I mean, I'm valuable to vampires. I am my own bargaining chip. If we can get out of this hellhole, and back to the Synedrion, I can leverage that value. I'm sure of it."

Owen seemed to ponder that for a moment. "You always were a clever one, Strawberry. Now, let's focus on getting away from the Starved, and whatever it is they want with us."

"Looks like we're about to find out," I said.

A small group of Starved stood before the bars of our cells. They had arrived silently, and the dim light and tattered brown robes camouflaged them until the last moment. The leather masks that covered their faces and heads were clearly hand-stitched, and the leather was badly cured so it was hard and cracked rather than soft and supple. The pieces that formed the hoods were crudely cut and stitched, much like their mouths. I shuddered.

One very large figure stepped forward, easily seven feet tall, and burly. He wore neat, black robes with gold embroidered edges, and no mask covering his bald head.

His skin had a strange ashen cast but wasn't desiccated like that of his brethren. No stitches bound his mouth. His eyes were the strangest part though, a bright, burning red rather than the pitch black all other vampires that I'd seen had. He clearly wasn't starved the way the others were, but they followed him like he was a leader. I wondered what he ate. I heard Owen inhale sharply at the sight of him.

"Bring her," he said, his voice like gravel.

My cage was unlocked. Masked Starved came for me. A hand, so skeletal it didn't resemble anything living, lifted and reached for me. I screamed and

scrambled away, but that arm caught my hair and yanked me forward. Pain traced along my scalp.

"Leave her alone!" Owen shouted.

They dragged me out. I bucked, but couldn't free myself as more hands grabbed and lifted me. My eyes turned to the stone wall that separated my cell from Owen's. I heard him thrashing against his cage.

"I'll be okay. It will be okay. I'll escape and find you," I cried out my lies, not knowing if they were for him or for myself, as I was dragged away.

12

KAITLYN

Tunnels turned this way and that as I was carried aloft by the Starved, led by the larger one. I tried to keep track; memorize the turns we took. Left, then right, then right again, then I was lost. The thought I couldn't find my way back to Owen if I had to filled me with helplessness.

We reached a huge cavern, lit by dozens of flaming torches. At least a hundred Starved filled the room, some still coming in from a number of other entrances. As we entered, they parted, and I saw what was behind them.

I wished I hadn't.

A monstrous stone statue of a giant demonic creature stood at least two stories tall. The face carved onto the creature was the stuff of nightmares:

bulging eyes, an obscene, lolling tongue, a horned forehead and an uneven grin, all made from a chalky, bone-colored stone, stained with patches of muddy red.

It had a bulbous body, and huge, gnarled claws, out of proportion with the rest of its size. Its misshapen feet were planted solidly behind a long stone altar. I gagged and turned away, not sure what it was I was seeing but knowing it was evil. So evil that there was no way to deny the darkness flowing from it.

I was dragged before the altar. The leader stood beside me on the raised dais, holding me up by the scruff of my neck to display me before the legion of Starved.

His grimy thumbnail moved along my face. I fought, my hands balling into fists, wanting to strike away that thing, but I was still restrained.

A thin sliver of pain came to my cheek. A wet and warm fluid dripped down my face. Blood! I cried out, despair and fear causing me to lose my courage.

The leader sniffed and the others leaned in, a low moan rippling across the room. The hoods showed their eyes but not their noses or mouths, and I watched with disgust as those leather masks moved up and down, and their eyes closed as they inhaled the aroma of my blood, like wine lovers sniffing their favorite vintage.

He spoke. "Yes, it is she of the strawberry blood."

Remortality

A strange howl arose from the crowd, muffled by mouths stitched closed.

"Kissare's chalice always delivers truth. Though others have long since lost faith, we remain. They succumbed to the thirst like fools. We remained, and here, now, is our reward."

If I thought that sounded bad, what he said next left my stomach on the floor.

"We have found the strawberry blood and the cured one. We have found the ones who will give us the child that will cure our thirst forever."

That throaty howl called out again, louder than before.

My instincts said to run, but there was nowhere to go. Nowhere to escape to. No way to break the hold of the hands on me.

I stammered, "I'm not planning on having kids anytime soon, so I'd say you would be better off letting me out of here and checking back in about ten years, you know, when my career's more stable and I'm ready to do the parent thing." I had no idea what he meant or even what I was saying. I just knew I wasn't pregnant and had no intention of being, either. And as for curing thirst, my blood could already do that, in a way, child or none, but I wasn't sure that was information these guys already had, or I wanted them to have.

My words were ignored regardless.

A Starved entered, carrying high a large chalice made of tarnished silver inlaid with blood red agate. The hair on the back of my neck stood up as I watched the hooded figures of the Starved suddenly animate and then bow. They crowded close to each other, their robes pooling onto the floor by their bent legs and feet.

The red-eyed leader took the chalice when it was presented to him. It held a small amount of liquid, and the leader wiped his finger up my cheek again, collecting my blood he'd spilt and dripped it into the water.

A red glow shone from inside the cup.

He stared into the light. I was too short to see whatever it was he saw, to know whether this was some sort of stage trick, or if this chalice really spoke some truth only he could see. I feared what truth my blood might be telling him.

The leering grin on his face when he finally looked away was like the worst news I could hear. "Place her on the altar," he said.

The Starved that held me followed his order with swift obedience.

I was laid down on the cold stone. My feet and legs were held by too many hands to kick. My hands and shoulders were held down by more. Tears ran down my face as the leader ran his hand up my leg, over my thigh, pushing my dress up to my ribcage.

Then he revealed a wickedly sharp blade in one hand.

The ones holding me muttered and chanted. I hated them. I hated them so much, and when the blade found my arm, every one of my muscles tensed and waited for it to open my veins.

Only it didn't. It cut the contraceptive implant from within the soft underside of my upper arm. I ground my teeth at the pain as the leader moved away and another Starved applied a tight bandage.

The leader looked upon the blood covering his knife with a lust that curled his lips back.

He wiped the blood with his finger, then with rough swipes he drew something onto my bare abdomen.

"Three days," he declared to a reply of howls. Then he left.

The Starved lifted my battered and aching body. I was too numb to fight anymore. They carried me to a cell and then closed the door.

I sobbed silently. I had an idea forming in my mind, but it was awful, so incredible I couldn't manage to make it shape into the thing I was sure it was.

"Strawberry. Kaitlyn. Please, look at me."

I lifted my head. I could see his face! They had put me in a cell next to his on the other side than I was before, one that had no stone wall between us, only a grid of rusted metal.

I sagged forward. Owen's arms came through the bars and held me up. My face pressed into the space between them and tears rolled down my face.

He wiped my cheeks, stroked my hair. He didn't ask what had happened. I knew he wanted to know, that I needed to tell him, but I wasn't ready.

A single Starved appeared and pushed a metal tray through a horizontal slot in the bars. I guessed if I didn't move to take it, he would let the miserable-looking food fall to the floor, and once it did it would be entirely inedible.

I moved to the front of the cell and took the tray. The Starved left us. I brought the food back to where Owen stood. I said, in a shaking whisper, "It's just bread and … and maybe that's … I don't know what that lumpy orange thing is."

"Eat."

I shook my head. "Not if you don't."

Owen looked at the small meal. "You need it more than I do."

"The hell I do."

I broke the bread into two pieces, then took a share of the oddly-shaped and bright orange thing, which, as it turned out, was some kind of pickled vegetable. It wasn't good, but it filled the hole in my belly. The rest I pushed through to Owen.

Owen spoke softly, "I heard … some of that, down

the halls. What did he mean by three days?"

"I don't know exactly, but if I had to guess I'd say he thinks that's about how long it will take the birth control hormones to leave my system." I showed him my bandaged arm. His eyebrows dropped into a deep frown. "They said something about us, me, and the cured one, giving them a child to cure their thirst. Did a magic show with a glowing chalice and all."

Owen inhaled so sharply his chin lifted. He stepped back from the bars, his food untouched, and paced like a caged wild-cat.

"A glowing chalice?" he repeated.

"Yeah. Crazy, right?"

"A child?" he growled.

I could only nod. I'd acted brave, but my whole body felt wrong. My toes curled and my thighs felt greasy and dirty, and I wanted to wash the feeling of unwanted hands away.

Owen whispered, "I won't, Kaitlyn. I won't do that to you. I won't. We just won't."

I swallowed hard. "The leader, with his red eyes, whatever that's about—"

Owen grunted.

"He also did this." I lifted my dress. Owen bared his teeth as though terrified to see what I meant.

My stomach came into view and there, on it, my blood made the shape of an upside-down ankh, roughly covering the area and shape where my

ovaries and womb would be.

"A symbol for life. It's probably … probably just symbolic," Owen said, his head shaking. "But that leader, he's … if his appearance is true, he is something else. Something even vampires consider a dark fairy tale. A vampire who is able to feed on other vampires. And if the chalice you saw is Kissare's chalice, we're past the realm of even normal vampire lore. These are things from myth and legend."

My own teeth clenched, and I spat on the hem of my dress and scrubbed the blood off my belly. I sank to the ground, sitting on the moist dirt.

"Just when I thought things couldn't get worse with the Synedrion, here we are with magic chalices and a cannibal super vampire who wants me pregnant." My forehead bumped the bars. "I mean, really, we're not even near rocks and hard places and frying pans and fires anymore. We're way beyond that."

Owen's hands came through the bars and my fingers wound around his.

I picked up the remaining bread and brought it to Owen's mouth. I knew it was the only way to make him eat. Even then he turned away at first, but finally took a small bite. He took it off me, feeding the next bite to me, then taking another for himself, the two of us sharing nibbles at the stale crust until it was gone.

Time ticked by, but there was no way to measure it. It drew out and on. The light stayed the same, and the stone walls had no chinks we could find.

We did look. We tried everything we could to escape. Not just because we wanted out of there but to pass the time. I knew, deep down, that the three days the shaman had given us would come to an end far too soon, but I still needed to keep my mind and body distracted.

Owen tried to dig at the softer parts of the rough walls with the metal tray our food had come on, and I used a rock that came loose to try to bash open the hinges of my cell door. We searched every crack in the stone and weld in the bars for weaknesses. Our only hope came when Owen unearthed a short length of partially rotten tree root in the back wall of his cell. It took him half a day of sharpening the side of the tray to be able to cut through the inch-thick wood and extract it, and another day of cutting and whittling to create two stubby wooden stakes. The wood was split and soft, barely long or rigid enough to form a point, but it was something.

Those pathetic stakes were what kept me from thinking about what would happen to me, to us, when the three days ended and whatever it was the Starved had planned for us came. I held tight to mine, and to one desperate hope.

Owen, my human, non-vampire Owen, would never force himself upon me. Never.

13

KAITLYN

I woke to a hollow gonging sound. My eyes snapped open as the sound infiltrated first my dreams and then my waking mind. The pungent, rotting, muddy smell reminded me exactly where I still was.

I was worn down by hunger and the filthy conditions of the cell. My body was a welter of bruises, and so was Owen's. We had no beds, only hard stone benches, and we were often blasted out of sleep by nightmares and fear.

The only thing I'd been able to think about was what if I did get pregnant. Or how long it might take to fall pregnant, and if this torture would not stop until I was.

And then what?

Would they hold me here in this filthy cell until

I birthed a child? Our child?

I couldn't stop imagining nightmarish futures. My heart twisted painfully as I wondered what they would do to that helpless infant once they had it. Surely, they wouldn't kill us, not until they knew for sure that whatever purpose that infant was intended to serve would be fulfilled, but once they knew that child was what they wanted, then our use would be finished.

And our baby? Would it be some kind of blood sacrifice for them?

My eyes closed to try to block off the image of my child, our child, being drained dry by those creatures. I couldn't escape the vision though. It stalked me even in the darkness of sleep. I could see my unmade child's feeble fists waving, hear its pained screams, feel its terror and misery.

My eyelids parted. Owen stared at me through the bars. I looked at his face, and I knew those visions of our potential future tormented him too.

We both were victim to the same nightmare, and we both understood exactly why we had to fight again, and again, and again to stop them getting what they wanted from us.

If only we weren't so weak.

We weren't fed often or enough, and I might have given up and cried over that hunger if Owen hadn't whispered to me wonderful things about the food we would eat when we finally escaped. Of handmade gnocchi drenched in burnt butter and sage sauce. Of lavender crème brûlée and light-as-air meringues. Of pork crackling, spiced with fennel seeds, so puffy it crumbled on our tongues.

It should have made me hungrier, his speaking of food when I was so famished, but it didn't. It soothed me because those things were so close—all we had to do was get out of that house of horrors.

And we would get out. We had to. I just didn't know how.

We had tried to overpower one of the Starved who brought our food, and Owen still wore a violently purple bruise on his cheek for that, while I had several shallow cuts in my left forearm from the loathsome creature's nails. Still, that attempt had given us fresh courage, even if it had failed.

The gong sounded again. The Starved arrived. They had come for us. Three days had passed, and it was time.

The leader stepped to the front, stood in front of Owen's cell, and a smile, one of sheer triumph, filled his face. His red eyes flashed, and Owen swayed on his feet.

I shouted through the bars, "Owen! No. He's enthralling you. Fight it!"

Too late. It was fast and easy, too easy. Owen had never stood a chance. I didn't even know if humans

could resist being mesmerized. I'd managed to with Owen once, but they were extenuating circumstances. Still, I'd expected more from a man who knew all about the dangers of a vampire's power.

One of the Starved opened his door. Owen, obedient as a thrall, stepped out.

The leader came to my cell next. I blocked off my mind, refusing to be compelled. Maybe I could beat it when Owen couldn't. My anger would be like a fire that burned away the Starved leader's attempts.

My lips pursed. Spit flew out of them and landed on his face.

The leader's fingers flicked it away casually, but I saw a glow of anger in his eyes.

"Bring her. Let her be aware for what is to come. We only need him to act."

Owen stood there, his face as smooth and blank as the visage of a statue as I was dragged from my cell, all attempts at mesmerizing me done and over with that spit bomb I had hurled.

The moment both I and Owen were out of our cells, Owen roared and launched himself at the Starved holding me. My heartrate soared with hope and adrenaline.

Wow. I wasn't the only one with decent acting skills.

There were only four Starved there, plus the leader. We were both free from our jail. We had a chance.

Owen pulled his stake from where it was held in the back elastic of his boxer shorts.

I reached under my dress and pulled my stake from the hem of my underwear and plunged it into the Starved dragging me from my cell. His dry flesh was hard, and splinters bit into my palm as I forced the stake in.

I was let go. The Starved stumbled back from me, then crumbled to dust, leaving my stake on the floor a few steps away. I dove for it, but I was snatched away by the burly leader. He scooped me up as though I were nothing. No matter how I bucked and struggled, his grip remained firm.

I was dying to stab this guy. I'd lost my stake, but Owen still held his.

I searched for him in the melee. He fought like a raging tiger, jamming a thumb into the eye of one of the Starved. It made a sickening popping sound, and sludgy blood flowed out of the mask. Still reeling from that, Owen staked him.

Two dead Starved was a good thing, but not enough.

Both my wrists were caught up in the huge hands of the leader. I struggled but couldn't free them. The leader didn't seem concerned about any of this.

Owen managed to drive the stake right into the back of another Starved, and I screamed with both joy and disgust before I was dragged away toward

the ritual chamber, toward that baleful statue.

More Starved poured down the hallway behind us toward Owen. He was up against a full dozen now, and alone.

I thrashed in the leader's hands, helpless as I lost sight of Owen. I could still hear him fighting as I landed on the altar, my arms bloody from the leader's brutal nails.

Starved filled the large cavern. Some moved to take over restraining me as the leader let go.

Owen was half dragged into the chamber, half fought his way in, trying to reach me.

I heard the blows he landed but I was held in place, spread-eagled and helpless, on that stone altar by both ropes and hands, and unable to assist him. One of the Starved made the mistake of getting too close to my mouth and I bit the bastard through his robes, sending him scrambling backward with a yelp.

I twisted and heaved my body up and down, hoping to slip through their fingers. My heels drummed against the stone slab.

Owen was fighting a losing battle, and he was tiring now. He no longer had a stake in his hand. His shoulders were slick with sweat and his chest heaved, but when the leader approached him, again Owen's fist came up and out and he delivered a devastating uppercut that stunned the leader for a moment.

As much as the idea of being alone terrified me, a moment of clarity hit me. I shouted, but it came out like a hoarse whisper, "Run, you should've run!"

I managed to get one wrist up and off the table a few inches. I grabbed the hood of the nearest Starved and yanked him toward the stone altar. His head hit it with a satisfying crunch, but it barely affected him.

The leader brought a hand down hard on Owen's shoulder. Owen's knees buckled under the force, and he was pushed onto them. The leader stared down with a force so powerful I could feel the energy coming off him in palpable waves that battered against my mind and body.

Owen went lax and limp under the leader's hand.

I began to weep because I knew this time it wasn't a ruse. I knew what was going to happen.

I could take it.

I could.

But could Owen?

The guilt of what he'd done to me in the past weighed so heavily on him. And he'd vowed, over and over, to never wrong me like that again. This could crush him.

I was pinned fast to the table. One of the Starved fastened my neck, strapping it down with rope so that I couldn't lift my head even an inch.

My teeth clenched together so hard they ached.

The leader drew closer, bringing Owen with him. Even though I was bound fast I could feel myself retreating from him. Not physically. But in every other way possible. My mind wanted to go blank. I wanted to disconnect as much as possible, and find a place where I could hide from the things that were about to happen to me, and to Owen.

I didn't allow myself that comfort. Owen needed me, more than ever. Now that he was human, he was ruled by the empathy and guilt that vampires didn't have. Humans couldn't deal with their emotions well, and a centuries-old vampire who had suddenly found himself human and burdened with human emotions again so recently was even less likely to be able to handle the guilt and confusion that this ritual would place on his shoulders.

So I didn't escape. I stayed with him, focusing all of my will and attention toward him. They would not break us. I wouldn't let them.

After the chaos of fighting, the space had stilled.

A low, muffled chanting rose in the room. It grew louder, and Owen climbed up onto the foot of the altar. His features shimmered as though caught under a heat haze, twisting and reshaping themselves. He was fighting, trying to break that spell. To save me from the ritual that would be forced upon us.

He jerked and moved like a puppet trying to fight its master. His fingers worked and he removed his only clothing, his boxers, as docile as a lamb. I pleaded with him, trying to help him escape the enthrallment. My words didn't even provoke so much as a blink from Owen.

I might as well have not even existed.

He stood above me, the outside of his feet touching the insides of my calves. The leader shouted at him to begin, but Owen didn't move. He was still fighting off that spell, and while I knew he would eventually lose and surrender, my heart swelled with love for him.

His courage gave me courage. His strength gave me strength. He made me want to keep fighting too.

Tears ran down my face. "This changes nothing, Owen. Can you hear me? I still love you. I know you aren't doing this because you want to. I know you wouldn't do it if you had any choice at all. This is not you or me right now, not really. I love you, and I will always love you."

Tears rolled down his blank face and splashed onto the altar.

The Starved paused for a moment, the chants falling away into a pin-drop quietude. The lull made goosebumps rise all over my skin. An expectant tension, heavily weighted with something else, something indefinable, fell over the gathering. My eyes rolled back and I stared up at the carved stone face of the demon statue that I lay at the feet of. I

was so sure the thing was coming to life, that for a moment, I could've sworn I saw it move.

Owen's teeth bared in struggle, and more tears leaked from his extraordinary blue eyes. The taste of salt lay in the corners of my mouth.

"I love you, Owen. I love you. I know you can hear me. This is not your fault, and I don't blame you, not for this. Never for this."

With a strange, wobbling, struggling motion, he landed on his knees on the altar.

Screams, earsplitting screams, rang out.

My heart stopped as those screams filled the room and I stared up at Owen, frozen above me.

Liquid splashed onto me. A cold liquid fell over my body, slick and sticky. That liquid touched my lips, and my mouth opened both in thirst and confusion.

Sweetness and the tang of anise met my tongue. *Absinthe?*

The Starved who held me down recoiled, screaming hard enough I could hear their stitches popping.

I turned my head to find out what was happening.

Heavy gray-green tendrils of smoke rose from the Starveds' robes, and one, who had been caught directly on the hood by the water, screamed and beat his head with hands that clicked and chattered like bones.

The leader snarled, stepping away as spots of wormwood-infused alcohol splashed his face and hissed and sizzled.

How did it just start raining absinthe inside? I looked for the source. The Starved whose robes were in flames whipped them off to reveal corded, sinewy flesh pulled over muscle that had shriveled and wrapped around hard edges of bone.

A few of the Starved lay dead on the ground, their robes wrinkling as their bodies crumbled away beneath them. More were falling back from a second explosion of green liquid, clearing away completely from the altar. I tried to swivel my neck to see where it was coming from but couldn't because of the way I was bound.

"Owen!"

That cry had not come from my mouth. My eyes went to the left, and a fierce, triumphant joy battered its way through my heart as I saw Lance striding through the altar room, a plastic container in one gloved hand and a hose that was attached to the container in the other. He pumped the handle again but nothing came from the tube.

The Starved also saw that he was out of ammunition. They were regrouping, like a swarm of ants.

Lance half jumped, half flew, to us. He yanked Owen down, and off the altar. His eyes flicked between the ropes binding me, and the Starved that were advancing on us. Owen, lax and unresisting, hung there in Lance's arms. Lance looked at him and

cursed under his breath.

The Starved growled and hissed, creeping closer to us again. The leader stalked forward in huge strides.

When Lance saw him and his glowing red eyes, he froze momentarily. "That better not be what I think it is."

I wrenched at the remaining ropes that still held me down. "Get me out of here!"

"What do you think I'm trying to do?" Lance said. He ripped the ropes binding one of my legs free, then looked again at the horde surrounding us. He was clearly stronger than them individually, but not all of them together, and once that massive, over-powered leader joined in, he'd be finished.

Lance took a step back from the altar. "There's too many. I can't carry both of you. I'm sorry."

Ice grew inside my heart.

I couldn't run fast enough on my own to escape this place. I knew what Lance had to do, and so did he, yet he hesitated.

I looked him in the eye, my jaw shaking. "Go. They won't kill me. Just get him out of here. You can't let them have us both."

Lance nodded firmly, holding Owen tight under his shoulder. He made a leap for the exit, carrying Owen with him.

They landed in a clear section, halfway to a tunnel leading out. The Starved pivoted, moving for them immediately.

"Run!" I screamed.

Owen jerked as though he'd heard me. He looked back at me, his teeth clenched. In control of his own body again, he fought against Lance. He struggled within Lance's grip, fighting with the same desperation and rage that he had fought the Starved with. He screamed, "We're not leaving her! You can't do this!"

"We have no choice!" shouted Lance.

Owen tried to break free. He did, once, and raced toward me, toward the wall of Starved between us, but Lance caught him in a bear hug and tugged him away. Lance was relentless, and far too powerful for Owen. He dragged him backward. He leaped again, and they disappeared down the tunnel.

"Kaitlyn!" Owen's final cry held sorrow so vast that it echoed along the walls and made my heart clench painfully.

Owen had been saved. Our potential child had been saved.

I was alone.

14

KAITLYN

I lay there on that altar, as still as the stone it was carved from.

My heart raced fast enough to cause a loud thrumming in my ears. But I barely even breathed. I stared with wide, dry eyes up at the cavern ceiling, willing myself not to cry.

I'd told them to go. It was their best chance, *our* best chance. It made sense.

I wished they didn't go.

The leader yelled in his coarse and guttural voice, "Go after them. Bring them back!"

I didn't move, but I heard more and more of the Starved dashing down the tunnel after Lance and Owen. Lance was faster than them, but dragging an unwilling Owen along with him had to slow him

down. I didn't even know if they went down the right tunnel. I didn't know which of the three tunnels into the chamber was the way out. I didn't know where we were. I didn't know anything.

I could only hope they would escape. And that they would come back for me before it was too late, before whatever horror was going to happen next.

The room grew quiet. Almost all the Starved were on the chase, but the leader stood above me, brooding.

I drifted my gaze down to meet his and found the ability to smile, a wild, triumphant smile.

"You can't do anything without him. You might as well let me go." I managed to inject some real authority into my voice. "Once Lance and Owen get back to the Synedrion, tell them what's going on here, you're going to be in big trouble. I hope they stake you out in the sunlight on top of a fire ant hill."

His burning red eyes looked down at me. Firelight glistened off his hairless scalp. He calmed, and that calm was more frightening than his rage. His huge hand with those filthy, sharp nails, wrapped around my throat.

"You will not escape your fate. You cannot. It has been seen by Kissare's Chalice as truth."

His hand clenched, enough to make me wince as breathing and swallowing became harder. "This setback means nothing. Either the cured will be captured and returned, or we use another way. There is another way. One of much greater sacrifice. Regardless, when the moon rises again, the child will be conceived."

I didn't like the sound of sacrifice. Surely they weren't going to kill me. They needed my uterus too much, didn't they?

In a cold, logical way, I considered that they could cure another vampire from my blood. But that took time, if it worked the same way again at all. I'd be safe from that outcome, for a while at least. They had to be planning something else.

The leader released his grip and left me lying there, bound on the malevolent altar.

The chamber was empty now except for me.

Now they all were gone, tears and a very real fear washed over me, and I screamed and sobbed for myself until my throat was raw.

Owen would come back for me. I knew that. He wouldn't leave me there to suffer. He knew now where the lair was and he would come back. I clung to that thought, because it was the only thing I had to comfort me. The stone of the altar bruised the hard points of my shoulder blades and tailbone. My ribs ached from not being able to take a deep and satisfying breath past the uncomfortable constriction of the ropes they had bound me with.

The sweet absinthe that had fallen into my mouth

had merely awakened my thirst. I concentrated on that thirst, reveled in it, because it meant that I was still alive.

I was alive and Owen had escaped.

There was hope.

There was worry too, of course. Would the Starved catch up to Lance and Owen? Would Lance be caught in the sun? Where would Owen and Lance go? Back to the Synedrion? Would they listen to Owen's story, or decide it was time to kill him after all? Would they come to help me, or come just to be sure I was finished off as well?

Owen did have some friends among those vampires. Perhaps, if he couldn't talk the Synedrion council into a rescue, he could convince some of those he had once called friends into helping us. Maybe he could even get the ones who wanted a taste of my blood on our side by offering me up to them in some way.

If they would rescue me, I'd be happy to fill a punch bowl with my cursed blood. They could have some, by all means. I'd rather lose a little than all of it, and what was a little blood between friends? They would be my friends too, if they would just come and get me out of here!

Despite telling myself that Owen would come back, that he would never leave me, no matter what, desolation set in. I tried to fight it back. It came anyway, and with it came a sense of deep loss.

Remortality

I could feel Owen's absence. Not just because I was now alone in that torture chamber, either. I felt the loss of him as keenly as though Lance had removed my left arm and taken it with him. All doubt was gone. I loved Owen with a depth that ached for every step he was away from me.

I couldn't just lie there, dwelling on how bleak things were. I had to try to get out of these bonds. I kept trying to yank my neck forward enough to loosen the rope, reasoning that I might be able to chew my way out of one of the straps holding down my hands if I could. And if I could get one hand out, I might be home free.

Eventually, I realized that the bonds holding my shoulders and neck in place were not coming loose, and my tugging and pulling at them was only resulting in chafed and painfully abraded skin. Talk about a pain in my neck.

I concentrated on the ropes around my arms and wrists. I kept tensing and loosening my muscles, hoping to feel even a slight slip. I braced the foot of my free leg against the top of the altar and pushed against it. Every move hurt. I knew when I had done too much because small trickles of blood began to pool around my wrists.

I kept going anyway. Maybe the blood would act as a lubricant.

There was a small yielding in the ropes.

I closed my eyes to the pain, gasping out harsh screams each time I strained against the rope, and it cut farther into my wrists. But they were moving, becoming looser. I almost had one hand free.

Then something rough touched my neck.

My eyes snapped open.

One of the Starved leaned over me, the hood hanging close to my neck. Her mask was off, and I could only just tell through the flaking and dehydrated skin that it was a her.

The Starved sniffed me and moaned with desire.

"Oh no, you don't. You can't. You're not supposed to drink. You'll be punished."

With pinched fingers, she tugged away the stitches in her lips, each one making a snapping sound as it broke. A reptilian tongue, dry and scraping, darted across the blood on my neck. A long, indrawn breath followed, and my insides froze as I looked sideways to see the Starved one licking her lips and shivering with the same sort of greedy abandon I knew I had displayed at fine restaurants.

Her tongue came back out and licked at my neck again. I pressed myself flatter into the altar, my throat knotting with a scream it was too sore to utter.

Despite my revulsion, I realized this could work for me. I hoped she did drink from me. I hoped she fed on me and felt some human emotion that would make her let me go, let me live. That would make her help me instead of the group she was part of, and if she had to bite me to have that happen, so be it. I braced myself for the touch of her dry lips against my skin, for the feel of sharp fangs puncturing my flesh and blood being taken.

A shout rang out. "How dare you?"

The Starved was yanked off me, thrown backwards.

The leader's hand lifted the one who had licked my neck off the floor and shook her like a ragdoll. The female Starved went limp. "Great Scarl, Forgive me. Her blood calls, you know it does, even more than normal. I couldn't resist. After so long in hunger, I couldn't resist!"

Scarl? Is that his name, or the name of what he is? He was definitely something … different. A vampire that drinks the blood of other vampires, Owen had said. A monster to the monsters.

Scarl dropped the Starved one onto the floor. The surreptitious licker whined and groveled for a few more seconds.

Scarl gestured to a tray with a bread roll and bottle of water on the ground beside her. "I sent you here to do a simple task, and this is how you go about it? You do not deserve to be one of us."

He hauled the Starved woman up off the floor and said, "I banish you. You cannot resist hunger, and if you cannot resist her here and now, then how will you resist centuries of starvation?"

The woman stuttered, her voice rough from who knew how long without use. "But with the child we shall never know hunger again. It shall slake the thirst forever. We will be immortal and without hunger. We're so close. Please, do not send me away now!"

My blood turns vampires human. Would my child's blood somehow allow them to still be vampires—but vampires who did not crave blood?

Immortal, all powerful, and no need to feed to stay 'alive,' for lack of a better word? I didn't know if that was a good or bad thing.

Owen had told me that many vampires sought ways to end their thirst. Many did not kill in order to feed, either because of moral reasons or because they didn't wish to risk turning a human who they drank from into a vampire. But they needed human blood, thirsted for it, and could only take that blood from living humans. Not the dead, not animals, not blood banks. No artificial method had yet been found.

The Starved didn't drink because they thought humans were below them, tainted. But they'd been promised a cure, through me, through my child, by some damned magic cup.

I had never wanted children. I wanted a career. I had never imagined having children before, and I wasn't sure I wanted to imagine it now, either, all things considered.

But the thought of bringing a life into the world, only

to have that life stolen by vampires, was unbearable. A motherly instinct that I didn't even know I had swelled inside of me.

Not all the Starved were on the chase, or perhaps some had returned, because a group of a dozen came at the leader's call. He spat out what the Starved woman had done, and they dragged her away.

My insides churned as Scarl cut away my bonds, then forced me back into the dungeon. He clicked his fingers, and another Starved appeared behind him, carrying the tray of food. He took the tough bread and tossed it at me like I was nothing more than a dog.

I caught it, because that bread was life, and there was no way in the world I was going to let it land on the filthy floor. I had to eat it if I was going to have any strength at all.

"No tray for you this time," he said.

I held my composure. "I need the water."

A small contemptuous smile tilted his lips into a sneer, and he threw the plastic bottle into the cell through the locked bars. I winced as it landed in the filth with a thump.

He left without another word. I wondered where the Starved woman was then. I had no idea if she was gone forever, or if she was somewhere in the place still begging for her spot in the cult. Or if they disposed of those who failed them in a more permanent manner.

My teeth closed on a hunk of bread and tore it away. I chewed, my jaws working hard and my teeth clicking and clacking, as though taking out my anger on them.

I picked up the plastic bottle from the ground. It was slick with mud, and I shuddered at the smell of it. I wiped the bottle as clean as I could with the hem of my also filthy dress, now a dark maroon rather than the bright fuchsia it was before. The bottle still felt wet despite being wiped and I stared at it, confused. Giving the soft plastic a gentle squeeze, a spurt of water came out from a pinpoint hole in the side.

My first thought was frustration. I needed every drop of water I could get. I unscrewed the cap and took a small swig, careful not to squeeze any more liquid out the puncture hole. It brought cooling and relief to my parched throat.

I stared at the bottle in my wet hands, and the tiny hole jabbed in the side.

It must have happened when it landed on the ground. But how?

I crouched over the area where the bottle had landed, and held my breath as I dug into the thick layer of filth with my broken fingernails. If my manicurist could see my hands now, she'd absolutely faint.

Something hard and smooth met my fingers through

the mud. A shard of glass. Pointed, and sharp down two sides like an arrowhead. I considered it a small miracle that I didn't slice a finger digging it out. And it was just the right size to conceal in the palm of my hand.

This was something. Something I might be able to use to cut through the ropes they bound me with if I was taken back to that horrible altar again. If I was left there alone. Something I could jab eyes or cut throats with. The idea left my hands shaking.

Get a grip. It was awful to consider these things, but I had to. I had to stay alive, and I had to get away from these monsters.

The glass shard gave me some hope, something to cling onto both literally and metaphorically. I used my loudest inner voice to tell myself I could use it to survive, trying to talk down all the other voices telling me I had no chance, even if I were armed to the teeth.

Hours passed. I had no way to know exactly how long. It felt like both an eternity and no time at all, but I knew night must come again soon.

I wound up on the floor with my arms dangling through the bars and jutting into the cell that Owen had occupied. His absence hit me again, and tears rolled down my cheeks. I needed him so badly. A hollowness had grown in my heart like a dark void, one that whistled a haunting tune inside of me.

I bowed my head and pretended that he was there, right there, that his lips were on the crown of my head, and he was whispering to me of ice-cold botrytis Semillon, handmade ganache truffles and sfinci fried ricotta filled with coffee cream.

I didn't know how long I sat there pretending. I did know that it probably saved my sanity in that moment. I had every reason to go insane. Every single reason.

And only one not to.

Owen.

15

OWEN

I came back into awareness with a jump. My blood pounded through my veins as I sat up, taking in my surroundings.

Stone walls, low thatched roof, moth-eaten curtains drawn shut with a faint glimmer of light showing through the gap in the middle. Dust on all the surfaces. Some abandoned farmer's cottage, maybe.

A scratchy woolen blanket had been thrown over my naked body.

Lance crouched beside me on the wooden floor. "I'm sorry I had to subdue you. You were fighting too hard. Slowing—"

He dodged my first fist and caught my second.

I roared at him. "You left her behind!"

Lance dropped my fist and ran his hand through

his silver hair. "I know. I hate it too."

"You have no idea ..."

"We only barely got away ourselves. Now we can get help."

Help. He just means our other imprisoners.

I wrapped the blanket around my waist and stood up, tearing through the room, throwing drawers and fabric aside until I found some old pants. I tugged them on. Too big, but they'd do.

Doing up the buttons, I said, "Where are we?"

"About halfway between Umbravallis and the Starveds' nest. A half hour's drive, or run, to either. No one knew they had an enclave so close."

"Then how did you find us?"

"I've fed from Kaitlyn. It made her easier to track." Lance didn't meet my eyes as he said that. "I would have come sooner, but I was suspected of helping you escape. They locked me up for two days, questioning me about it and Delphine's death. But Joss was half awake during your capture and saw the Starved take you. It took her a long time to shake off the full effects of the Nemexia, but once she did, she let me know who took you. She freed me so we could make our case to the Synedrion, but I ditched her and came on my own."

"They aren't going to like that," I said.

"The hell with what they like. They would have been still arguing now about what to do. Seems to me I barely made it in time.”

A deep, aching chill ran from the crown of my head all the way down my body to my toes. I hadn’t been able to control what I was doing, but I’d been there. I’d experienced it all. I’d fought against it, and I still hadn’t been able to stop.

I picked up a dust-grayed ceramic pitcher from the table and smashed it against a wall.

“You were under a thrall. What you were doing, whatever *that* was, it wasn’t you,” Lance said softly.

“Did you see their leader?” I asked.

Lance nodded slowly. “Do you think he really is a Scarl? A red fiend?”

I shrugged. “He has the traits supposedly possessed by one. He also has Kissare’s chalice.”

Lance’s jaw dropped then clenched. “You have to tell the Synedrion. Between the value of Kaitlyn to them, and the chalice, they will come to our aid.”

“Screw the Synedrion.” I turned to Lance, taking a fistful of his death-dusted shirt in my hand. “Turn me, brother. Make me one of you again. Give me the strength to save her.”

I saw my own reflection in the black pools of Lance’s eyes, my skin scratched and bloody and covered in grime. I saw my desperation. How I shook with despair and fury.

Lance saw it all too, and still he shook his head. “I will not. You have something precious. These feelings,

this love you have for her, and her love for you. You want to fight for that, but you'll lose it all if I turn you."

"They want her pregnant, Lance." I half sobbed out the words. "They want her child, prophesized by the chalice to take away their thirst. Do you realize what they could be doing to her?" *What I almost did to her?*

Lance gently detached my fingers from his shirt and held my hand in his, strong between us. "We'll save her. You don't have to tell me she is precious, that she's worth saving. I *know*. I want to save her too. But we need help. We need more than the two of us. That's why you're going back to the Synedrion, and you will convince them to help us."

"They won't," I said.

"You will have to find a way to make them. I'm stuck here for the day now. If the Starved were still on our heels, they would burn out there too. Whether they took shelter as well or went back, we're all stuck."

"I'm not," I said.

Lance watched me, warily. Dawn brightened the sky outside the cottage. If I ran, Lance couldn't follow, or he would burn out there.

"Take this time to get help. I've already called Joss; she's coming to collect you."

On cue, I heard the rumble of a car out the front. I cracked the curtain to see one of the Synedrion's driverless cars with opaque black windows.

Lance shied back from the shaft of light that lit the floating dust in the cottage.

If Joss was in that car, she wouldn't be able to come out to get me. Lance couldn't take me out to the car. Once outside, between the two of them, I could run.

But where? I couldn't even find my way back to the Starved without Lance, and I was helpless. Lance was right; we needed more help. I had to try to convince the Synedrion to send us aid. Somehow.

"I'll bring back help."

I opened the door carefully, and Lance stood behind it, guarded from the sunlight that streamed in.

"Tell them what has happened, about the Scarl, the chalice, their plans for Kaitlyn. They *will* listen this time, I'm sure," Lance said. "And remember, you killed the Starved that are dead back there. I killed none. Because the Synedrion will ask."

I nodded. Regardless of who it was or why, it was a serious crime for a vampire to kill another vampire. Serious enough to warrant being bound to the sun. To take an immortal life was considered something far worse than taking a mortal one.

Lance grabbed my shoulder. "I will stay here till night, but take comfort that one way or another, with or without the Synedrion, I will be going back for Kaitlyn."

I clapped my hand on his, then stepped outside. One way or another, I would be too.

16

KAITLYN

Anxiety conspired to turn me into a bundle of nervous energy. I paced the floor of my cell for hours. I couldn't sleep, despite knowing I needed it. I didn't know how long I had been awake at this point. It felt like days.

With every footstep or scuttling sound, my head swung to look. I kept expecting Owen to be thrown back into the cell next to mine at any moment, his escape failed.

My dark hair hung in scraggly matted sections, itching my skin. I pulled it back from my face, winding it into a bun as tight as the knot in my stomach.

The stale air of the cavern never felt like enough. I stared at the ceiling, wondering if there was a whole mountain above me.

I heard the key clanking in the lock, and looked over my shoulder.

The Starved had come for me again.

I hid the glass shard I intended to use to escape in the palm of one fist.

The door opened and they entered. My eyes went from one hooded and cloaked figure to the other. They seemed a somber bunch tonight. I could see the tension in their bodies, and they reeked of something reminiscent of old sweat and leaking batteries. It was weird and upsettingly familiar. It was the same way I had smelled when I first realized I was held captive by a real vampire who desired my blood.

That was the stink of fear.

The smell unsettled me so much I almost dropped the glass. Just in time, I curled my fingers around it, safe and concealed.

I sized up the group. When in the past they might have only been a few, this time, there was a full dozen to escort me. I didn't fight. Not yet. There were too many. It would be futile, and I'd lose my makeshift weapon in the process.

I walked out of the cell before they could grab me. They seemed happy to keep their hands to themselves. Maybe news of the banished one had spread. They led me through the long tunnel to the ceremony chamber.

The torches were all lit and flaming bright, but

the cavern was nearly empty. There weren't as many Starved as before. Around twenty or thirty. Maybe I'd have a chance, if the right moment came up.

I searched the raised area with the altar, where the leader stood. No Owen.

They hadn't caught him. Maybe they were still out looking. But those remaining seemed to be going ahead with Plan B regardless. Whatever that was.

I expected them to take me to the altar and tie me down upon it, the way they had done the last time they had trotted me out for a ritual.

But they paused. Other than the shuffling of feet, they remained quiet. No chanting, no howls of victory.

It was eerie, and it was frightening. They stood there, holding me by my arms but not moving. The hands clasping my flesh never warmed no matter how long they stayed against my skin, and no matter how long they were against my skin I could not seem to accept them being there.

My brain kept dancing around the question—if Owen wasn't here, what were they planning to do?

I felt the way I had the night of the LARP game that had delivered me into Owen's possession.

A deep gut instinct that something was wrong.

Something that was right there in front of my face, and if I could just clear my head, really focus, perhaps I could see it.

When I'd agreed to take the LARP job, I'd been too busy worrying about how to get a part, how to make something out of the nothing that I had. I'd only thought of the money promised for that night's work, and the need to find a new agent. I had been worried about my broken-down car, and the fact that my rent was late, yet again, and I was facing eviction.

I'd been too busy focusing on all the wrong things. I didn't listen to my gut telling me the job was going to get me into trouble, that it was the kind of job girls might disappear from. But back then, I didn't have the knowledge to realize the risk wasn't one of sexual harassment, but rather ending up as vampire food.

Owen had told me it hadn't been his intention to drink so much from me, or to take me prisoner. He had said, a trifle sheepishly, it was not uncommon for him to arrange those reenactments so he could snack on the players and actors. He would always wipe the memory of those he drank from, but something of the emotion sometimes remained. And something of a nasty-looking love-bite. Taking his meals from those who'd been at a vampire re-enactment made things easier to explain.

It probably would've been business as usual if he hadn't sniffed my blood out. But it was my fault I was there at all. I let all those distractions cloud my focus and distract me from the truth that was lurking right beneath the surface.

And there was a truth here, now, as well.

A dangerous truth, that churned deep in my gut.

I was being distracted by the unusual quiet, the glass sliver in my hand, and my hope to use it as an escape plan, the feel of the Starved one's grip on my flesh, and the aching loss of being here without Owen.

There's a truth here, I said to myself. *Open your eyes to it right now, because whatever it is, if you don't see it coming before it happens, it may be the death of you.*

It had something to do with the ritual.

It had to, but what?

They wanted my child to cure their thirst.

They needed the cured one to impregnate me, but Owen was gone.

Owen was the only cured vampire.

My blood had made him human.

There was a connection there somewhere, I knew it, but I wasn't able to see it. I had been rendered punch-drunk by physical abuse, hunger and thirst, fatigue and the sheer mind-numbing amount of evil I had been subjected to.

Metal ground against stone, clattering down behind me. The tunnel we had come along had been closed by a thick gate of gridded, rusty bars. Each of the three tunnels that led into this chamber had been closed off.

Did they expect Lance to attack them again? Was this a precaution?

There was already movement behind the bars. A crowd of shuffling, silent bodies.

That was where the rest of the Starved were. But why were they locked out, only a fraction of their order in the ritual chamber?

The small crowd of Starved around me knelt in a neat line before Scarl.

He drew his ceremonial dagger and sliced down the pad of his thumb. Walking along the line, he anointed each of the Starved in the room on their foreheads with the bright red blood he let run.

Electric tension struck as he walked past me. I clutched my small piece of glass and wondered if it would be far better to plunge it right into Scarl's throat now, even if it meant my own death. With the whole room barred, and Starved inside and out, maybe death was my best option.

Scarl finished dabbing his blood on all the Starveds' foreheads. He took his central position and boomed in his crackling voice, "For your sacrifice, we are eternally grateful."

The anointed Starved placed both hands over their mouths then reached them toward Scarl. The Starved outside the chamber howled wordlessly.

They hoisted me up to the altar, and right past, to the huge, grotesque statue behind it.

Remortality

Ropes had been tied to the stone figure, and I was lifted into the air between them.

My wrists were bound by the two ropes hanging down, then the two ropes beneath me were lifted up, tying my ankles. I was suspended from my wrists, like a butterfly caught in a spiderweb. I was facing away from the statue, but leaned back enough that my view was filled with the disgusting hollow of the demon's mouth and its long, lolling tongue.

An uncontrollable, rattling fear built in me as it occurred to me that maybe, just maybe, they were going to attempt to bring that statue to some kind of impossible life, and have it impregnate me.

Struggling got me nowhere except re-opening the torn skin around my wrists. The wounds there burnt like the ropes were made of lava.

One of the Starved who'd bound me paused for a moment.

He took a long sniff of me, and a low growl began in his throat. It was the sound that a starving dog might make when it was about to fight for food. It sent spirals of cold radiating out from my center. My eyes went to my fist, curled around the glass so hard my skin broke. The warm sting of blood on cut flesh filtered into my awareness.

Had they seen it?

The one who had growled ran his dirty fingers over the abraded patches on my wrists and growled again. He thought the smell was coming from there and hadn't noticed my only weapon. I still had hope there would be a moment I could cut these ropes to free myself.

They worked again at the ropes at my ankles, pulling the tension tighter. The one who had growled seemed as disconcerted as I felt. He worked fast, sloppily, and every motion told me he was eager to get away from me. It was apparent that my blood was testing his hunger and thirst in a way he could not handle.

Good. As long as he was driven to hurry by the temptation of my blood, and the fact that it could cause him to break his vow and be exiled, he would continue to be sloppy while tying me up to the demon statue.

My hope strengthened when the Starved stepped away. I gave my wrist and ankle on the growler's side a quick little wriggle and found the ropes weren't as tight as the others. If I could get that hand and that foot free while they were busy with whatever ritual they were planning, I might have time to saw through the rope on the other side and free that hand too.

The leader spoke, "It is time for us to claim our destiny."

The sickening howls raised through the echoing cavern again.

Remortality

"I sacrifice myself." Scarl looked around the room at the Starved inside, and then at those outside the bars. "Those who die now, and the death I take, do so that our kind may never have to crave the unworthy blood of a human ever again. We die so they may live eternally, and live without hunger. We die so they may live in pureness and wholeness ..."

Giddiness, or maybe temporary insanity, set in. All of the Starved in the chamber with me were going to be some kind of sacrifice? Including the leader?

And I was, what? Hanging here to be some kind of spectator?

Whatever. I would be cutting myself free as they offed themselves.

I snarled at them. "Get on with it then. I'm more than ready to see the end of you all."

Despite being bound in the air a few feet off the ground, Scarl was tall enough to look me in the eyes. The blood red glow of his unsettled me. "You will not be free of me yet, vessel. I take the long death tonight, for my brethren. I take the death of mortality."

Bile rose in my throat so fast it made my eyes water.

The truth I didn't see. The truth I wouldn't see, hidden behind my foolish hopes, behind my own denial.

They didn't need Owen. They would use my blood to make another cured one.

And that cured one was going to be Scarl.

17

KAITLYN

My legs went weak, and had it not been for the ropes I would've fallen.

The starved leader planned to make himself human with my blood, to be the one to impregnate me. Acid filled my mouth and eyes, but hope came too. He would drink from me, he'd have to, again and again. It could take weeks. I had time.

But what were these other Starved for?

Scarl raised his arms high, and the twenty or so Starved within the room formed a circle around the statue. They climbed, one at a time, to the top of the statue's head. I couldn't see them once they got up there; I could only see the underside of the demon's face. But I heard horrible sounds. Cutting sounds, howling, slashing.

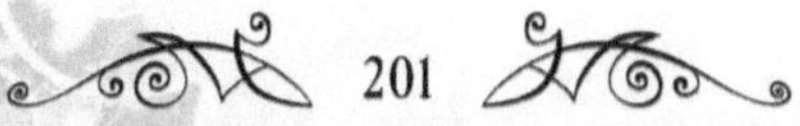

The demon's tongue seemed to move.

I blinked as something splashed onto me in a thin stream, cold, thick, and a dark, off-red.

Blood.

The demon statue wasn't moving. The appearance of movement was the blood, flowing through a channel in the demon's head, along its tongue, to create a waterfall of blood down to Scarl and me. The blood moved slowly, a thick slurry of scarlet. It flowed onto my arms and ran over my belly, soaking into the fabric. The tangy, earthy smell was overwhelming. The horror was equally overwhelming.

"No, no, no," I stuttered. But my denial couldn't stop it from happening.

The blood of twenty Starved dripped onto and around me.

The leader reached up his hands, chanting, catching the falling red rain. He cupped his hands, drinking their blood. It was true. He did drink other vampire's blood. His eyes lit with an inner glow, as though that blood set him on fire inside.

Throwing his shoulders back, he dropped his cloak away so it hung from where it was belted around his hips. He stood there painting his bared chest, face, and scalp with the blood of his brethren until he was red all over.

I stared, transfixed by terror. With a mental slap to the face, I shook myself out of it.

Remortality

A cold voice, a steely determination, spoke up in my head. *You can live through this. You can. It will be awful, but you can live through it. You lived through Owen when he was a vampire, and you can live through this too. You have to. You have to live, because death is the only other alternative.*

With Scarl busy chanting and finger painting himself, and the other Starved in the room bleeding out on top of the statue, it was probably now or never.

I worked my fingers into my palm to try to get a useable grip on the glass.

The glass slipped in my sweat. I grasped hard to catch it. The sharp tip jabbed into my skin, but I didn't drop it. I let out a silent *phew*.

My hands shook, numb from being tied so high over my head. My heart raced as I forced them to work. I pinched the glass between my thumb and forefinger and got it to the rope. I sawed furiously. Sweat broke out on my forehead and streamed down my cheeks. I licked it away from my lips and kept going, blinking back stinging drops of perspiration from my eyes.

The rope barely frayed.

My wrist and arm ached, seized up, and I hadn't done much more than cut away a few strands of the rope.

The leader roared. I thought he'd seen my escape attempt, but he paid that no attention. His fangs

were bared, his muscles straining and obscene under their coating of red gore.

The Starved outside the barred entrances were going crazy, clamoring against the gates, howling and grunting through sewn lips.

Scarl ripped my dress open down the front. He placed his hands on my stomach, leaving bloody handprints there, and then with a growl, sunk his teeth into my neck.

I cried out, horror and pain making the edges of my vision dance and blacken.

He detached himself quickly, and I wondered for a moment if he'd changed his mind. If my blood was changing him. But those thoughts vanished when he chanted more words, then stabbed his fangs back into the other side of my neck, drinking deep.

His lips already felt warmer. He was becoming human much faster than Owen had. This ritual was somehow speeding up the process. The part of me that had hoped I had time was crushed, but the fight didn't leave me.

I kept sawing at my bonds. Scarl was too focused on drinking and chanting to notice.

Blood flowed down from both sides of my neck as the leader paused to chant then drink again, over and over.

Those locked out of the room were going nuts, the smell of my blood flowing, and their leader, quickly becoming human, too much for their craving, empty bodies. They threw themselves at the bars, wrenching at them, clawing at the stone. The sound of groaning metal and crumbling rock made me work my piece of glass faster.

If the Starved out there broke through, it was only me and an almost human in here. They would overwhelm us. They would tear us to pieces in their hunger. I could hear it in their frenzied howls.

Only the leader showed restraint, drinking from me bit by bit between the dark, incomprehensible words he spoke. I wondered if he hated it, if it disgusted him, having to drink from a thing he thought so little of.

Or maybe he was just being very careful to keep me alive. All of this would be for nothing if I died.

At least it meant I remained lucid enough to keep fighting. One of the larger strands of rope snapped under the glass, my arm jerking almost free. Just one thin fiber to go.

Scarl gurgled out a deep cry, and staggered a few steps. His head fell back, exposing the long curve of his throat. He bellowed, an undulating howl that made the hair on my arms and the back of my neck stand up.

Scarl's skin rippled, then it went shiny and glowed bright red. His arms shot out and his fingers flexed and curled. The nails he had retreated, growing backward right into his nail beds.

He fell onto his knees, clutching at his heart. His body shuddered. Blood spilled from his mouth and nose. His head came back up, red streaming down his face. His chest moved, his ribs expanded and contracted as he took deep breaths in newly working lungs.

I looked into his eyes, hoping to see a shred of humanity there, something I could speak to. His eyes were hateful, a bright red-brown that looked at me with contempt. Regaining his humanity had done nothing for his personality. *Once a fanatic, always a fanatic.*

He rose to his feet with a look of determination. I met his stare, equally determined. The two of us alone in the center of the room, both drenched in blood. He was still huge, stronger and larger than me, but we were both human now.

I put all my strength into one final tug at the rope I'd been cutting, and my arm swung free.

I cried out in pain as the movement ripped at my bleeding wrists and throat. I fought through the pain. I had to, while I still had the advantage of surprise.

I slashed at Scarl with the blade of glass, aiming for his vulnerable, human throat.

He moved at the last second. The glass went deep into his cheek, exposing a vast flap of muscle and tissue below his skin. It also cut the skin between my fingers, and blood flowed down my hand onto my wrist. My fingers went slick and I lost my grip on the glass. It dropped away, my only weapon and my only chance gone with no way to get it back again.

His shock turned to wild fury. He backhanded me in a way that made my head ring.

A loud cracking sound followed by an enormous crash of thunder struck the air.

My thoughts blurred. *How can I hear thunder down here in the cavern?*

Stars in my eyes, thunder in my ears. My thoughts dulled then cleared.

It wasn't thunder.

It was the sound of the Starved breaking down the bars.

18

KAITLYN

Real fear filled the leader's eyes as the Starved flowed into the chamber.

"Stop this!" he roared. "Fight your hunger! It will ruin everything when we're so close!"

And I did see fighting. The crowd of Starved tumbled over each other, fighting to be the first to reach us, fighting each other. Some appeared crazed for a taste of blood; others tried to hold them back. Black shadows darted between them, strange blurs like moving darkness that made me distrust my eyes.

Two Starved broke free of the crowd and rushed at the altar. They ripped off their hoods, their nails tearing the stitches out of their skin with sickening popping sounds that turned my stomach.

Scarl reached into his robes hanging from his

hips, and drew his ceremonial dagger. I bet he was wishing he had some stakes right about now.

I knew I was.

I didn't even have my glass shard anymore. And I only had one arm free.

Scarl sliced the throat of one Starved right through, decapitating it. Its headless body stumbled back from him and turned to dust.

Another reached me, fangs first, tearing deep into my thigh. I beat at his wrinkled face with my free fist, but was too weak to detach him.

Then he became a shower of dust that stuck to the tacky blood on my skin.

Behind that dust stood a figure all in black.

An Ebonguard? My heart burst into breakneck pace. Then stopped, when I saw who stood there as well.

Owen.

I sobbed in sheer relief, sagging and hanging from the ropes.

His hands cupped my face. I could not lift my eyelids to see him. From the corners of my vision I saw Scarl, wrestling a Starved across the altar.

"Strawberry. Kaitlyn. Savior of my life. You're safe now."

My body didn't move but I mentally shook my head, denying what he said. Seeing him here, amongst all of this, snapped something inside of me. I wasn't safe. I would never be safe. He would never be safe. *We* would never be safe. This couldn't be true. I could feel myself tumbling into the yawning abyss of insanity. I could touch that madness. I could see its deep and seductive darkness right there, so close, hear it whispering that all I had to do was let go and this horror would go away.

But Owen's voice called to me, "Look at me. I'm right here and I love you. Come back to me. I'm begging you."

My lips cracked as I used all my last energy to whisper, "I love you too."

His fingers moved along the ropes binding me. Was I dreaming? Was any of this true? His body, so warm and alive, pulled me closer. I could feel the steady beat of his heart against my chest.

It was real.

He was real, and I was still alive.

He came back for me. Of course he did. And he brought help.

Ebonguard filled the room. They were the black blurs I'd seen before. I didn't know how many; they moved too fast to follow.

"Joss," Owen grunted, anguish all over his face. "Cut her down."

Joss nodded, and the ropes were sliced before I could blink.

I collapsed into Owen's arms. He caught me, and

bundled me up.

He almost toppled backwards as more Starved reached us, clawing at him. The room was in chaos, a bloody free-for-all. Joss's arms flashed, fighting three to her one. One Starved dragged its fingers across the armor around her throat, making a sound like nails on a chalkboard. It lashed out at her face, tearing away the black cowl she wore, revealing dark skin and bright pink hair.

Joss lashed back, her limbs an elegant flow of motion as she flipped two of the Starved to the ground. They were pinned there with metal stakes, right through their abdomens and into the stone. I was confused why they weren't being killed, and saw throughout the room more Starved pinned down like insects in a gruesome collection.

Owen ducked away from the third, still holding me. I wrapped my arms around his neck, pressing my body to his, as though I could melt into him, be shielded by him entirely.

The Starved who reached for us was grabbed by a hand on each shoulder, one from Joss, and one from Lance, who threw him onto the ground and pinned him down as well.

Joss and Lance formed a barrier between the Starved and where Owen held me. I wanted to press my face against his strong chest and not see what was happening in the room, but the clash of combat drew my gaze.

Blood and ash and screams filled the chamber. Some Starved tried to flee, but they were no match for the Ebonguard. Brown-robed bodies filled the room, pinned to the ground, squirming for freedom.

Still, the Ebonguard were not killing the Starved.

The Starved were killing themselves.

They were driving stakes into their hearts, or using ceremonial knives to release their thick, dark blood into the air and onto those nearby instead of being captured. I wept, not only out of horror but out of a kind of shocked pity at the sight. The Ebonguard were trying to capture them, but they were choosing to end themselves instead.

A movement near the altar caught my eye. The leader was there, sheltering himself behind the stone block. But he couldn't hide the scent of his now human blood. A group of his followers dogpiled him, and I heard his pained cries.

Lance broke away from us, throwing the skeletal bodies of the Starved off the leader into the crowd, where they were taken down by Ebonguard. He wrenched Scarl to his feet, his new human blood flowing freely from scratches and bites over the dried blood he'd painted on himself.

"You're not getting out of this that easily," Lance spat.

Joss surveyed the room. She whipped a black scarf from her belt and wrapped it around her face to

replace the cowl she'd lost. She signaled to another Ebonguard, who came and took the leader off Lance. In two blurred leaps, the Ebonguard and Scarl were out of the chamber.

"Give me Kaitlyn," Joss said. Owen hesitated, then nodded and passed me over like a child. Joss nodded to Lance who took hold of Owen. "Let's go."

19

OWEN

I wanted to keep hold of Kaitlyn. I never wanted to let her go again.

But there were still Starved and Ebonguard fighting out there, still Starved who could be lurking in the tunnels. And I was only human, too weak and slow to carry Kaitlyn out of this hellhole. So I handed her over.

Air rushed past as Joss and Lance sped us from the cavern, out of the stinking blood-addled darkness.

The air freshened as the cave tunnels became stone stairs, leading up through a house then out into freedom.

Cars lined the weedy dirt driveway. I turned my head to look back.

The house was plain and small, nestled in front of a rocky hillside, made of mud-bricks and with a thinly

thatched roof. It could have been any picturesque cottage sitting in a pastoral countryside.

How could such evil lurk beneath such an innocent-looking exterior?

Joss handed Kaitlyn back to me without ceremony. I thanked her silently.

A slim band of moonlight lay across the overgrown grass, full of singing insects.

I could feel Kaitlyn take a big lungful of that fresh air. I breathed deeply too, the tight compression of stress around my chest breaking as though it had been bound by leather straps. The smell of wildflowers, and something else, filled my nose.

"Look," I whispered to Kaitlyn.

Her gaze followed my pointing finger and stopped, staring at a low stone wall hung with leafy runners that bore ripe, red wild strawberries.

Tears washed trails through the grime and blood on her face.

Those strawberries said life existed beyond this death, and blood, and terror. That something beautiful and life-giving could grow even out of soil darkened by misdeeds and horrors.

"We're alive. We're really still alive?" Her voice was half sob, half whisper. Her hands reached for my face, as though trying to confirm I was tangible.

"We are," I said. I eyed the Ebonguard around us, preparing to take us back to the Synedrion. *But for how long now, I don't know.*

We had been delivered from this pit of horrors back to a cold, calculated verdict that would be made by the council.

Kaitlyn nuzzled her face into my chest, wetting it with her tears.

Joss waited by a black van, the back door open. I carried Kaitlyn over and stepped up and in with her. Inside was laid out like an ambulance, and the Synedrion's doctor waited, first-aid supplies at the ready.

I placed Kaitlyn onto the stretcher on one side. I had to pry her arms gently from around my neck.

Joss banged on the wall between our part of the vehicle and the front, and the van got into motion.

Kaitlyn lay flat with a sigh and opened her eyes. Looking at Ewan, she groaned. "It's my favorite doctor."

"I should be," he replied. "I'm probably going to save your life right now. Unless you'd like to die of blood loss and infection."

She deadpanned him. "Hmm, blood loss and infection, or your bedside manner. Both deadly. Do I really have a choice?"

"No," he said, and got to work. He moved as fast as he could, as fast as a vampire could, his arms a blur as he dressed Kaitlyn's wounds. She winced as he washed them with saline solution, and the sharp smell of antiseptic followed. He applied padding and

pressure bandages around her neck, crisscrossing her torso so it didn't restrict her breathing, then saw to her other abrasions, cuts, and puncture wounds. I noticed, as he flashed with motion, sample bottles being laid out behind him, blood wiped from Kaitlyn's skin.

Within a few minutes, Kaitlyn's wounds were all cleaned and dressed, and she was hooked up to fluids, antibiotics, and pain relief.

"Okay, maybe you are my favorite doctor," she said, as the codeine hit her system. Despite the clean patches around open wounds, her skin and clothes were stained in a layer of grime and dried blood. "Now I just need some water, a good meal, and about sixteen showers in a row."

I took her hand, kneeling beside the stretcher so we were eye to eye. I swallowed a hard lump that came into my throat. "I'm so sorry I left you there."

"Don't be. We might have both ended up dead, or worse, otherwise. And I don't think Lance gave you much choice." Her tears had stopped, and her breathing was strong and even again. *That's my Strawberry, so strong.*

I took some spare saline solution and gauze, and wiped the blood from her face where tears had left clear rivers in the dirty red layer. "I should have brought you clean clothes. I'm sorry I didn't think of that."

"You brought the cavalry. Way better." Kaitlyn tilted her head with a wince, looking for Joss. She reached a hand out, as though to touch her, or shake her hand, a gesture Joss ignored. "Thank you," Kaitlyn said.

"Just doing my job," Joss replied through the black scarf that covered the bottom half of her face. She looked away, as though staring into the distance, like she had no interest in us at all. Then her eyes flickered down to meet Kaitlyn's, and back away again. "You're welcome."

I couldn't help but smile. My Strawberry always did have a way of winning hearts, even the blackest of them.

I hoped that would be enough for what was to come.

20

KAITLYN

When our van pulled up outside the Synedrion's palace, my first response had been, "Oh, hell no! They want to kill us! They want to kill me! You rescued me just to take me back here?"

That was until I got inside, and got into the shower.

I must have stood under the hot jets of water for an entire hour, letting them wash away every last trace of the Starveds' torture cave from my skin, and hair, and soul.

Owen offered to join me, to help wash me since my arms still ached so much, but I wasn't quite ready for that kind of intimacy again. Not yet.

So I stood there, alone and still, under the running water, letting the warm stream wash me clean like tears of life.

When I finally emerged, I found Owen had left some clothes for me in the bathroom. Thick, fluffy socks, a soft merino hoodie, and comfy yoga pants. I gingerly peeled off the waterproof covers for my dressings that the doctor had provided, then slipped the clothes on. I cuddled the soft, clean fabrics to myself. They were like heaven.

A bath would have been heaven too. I'd planned on one at first, but Ewan said showers only, doctor's orders, as a bath would soak all the contaminants on my skin back into my cleaned wounds. I didn't like the sound of that much either. He said he had orders to draw new blood samples from me too, but would wait until I had recovered a little. He reminded me to hydrate, *again*.

Tomorrow I would have a bath. If my luck kept up and I was still alive then. Maybe being captured and tortured by hangry vampires, then held prisoner again by bureaucratic vampires, wasn't the kind of thing I'd normally consider lucky, but I still lived. Against all odds, I was alive. There had to be some kind of miracle work involved in that.

I stepped out of the bathroom and went through the bedroom into the living area. These were not the same quarters we'd been in before, which I was sure were undergoing a major clean and renovation after what had happened in there, but they were laid out in the same fashion. A huge and luxurious living area, and a separate bedroom and bathroom. I almost considered staying in the bedroom, lying down, and sleeping for days, but I could smell food beyond.

Owen had cranked up the heat in our room and I cuddled myself again, relishing the warmth and my still beating heart under my clothes.

Lance and Owen sat at a table together in front of one of the domed room-service-style trays. They both stood quickly when I entered the room, both moved to pull the chair out for me.

I walked to Owen, and Lance re-adjusted, reaching to open the food coverings instead. He cleared his throat. "I'm afraid, with all the time spent on rescuing, I wasn't able to bring in any more fine food for you."

Under the dome were two bowls of the thick stew given to thralls. "I will make sure you have better for breakfast tomorrow."

I didn't even blink—just grabbed a spoon and started eating. Right then, it was wonderful. Better than truffled triple brie on artisan lavash. Better than prosciutto-wrapped lamb backstrap, or stuffed and deep-fried zucchini flowers. Hell, right now, it was better than deep-fried anything, and that was saying something.

Owen had waited until I started eating, then joined me. Lance watched, his expression sharing both a small smile and a small frown. I noticed then an Ebonguard standing by the door, their

usual policy when it was more than just Owen and myself in the room.

"Joss?" I asked. I wasn't sure, but she looked to be the right height and build.

She gave a small nod.

"Come and join us," I said, patting the fourth chair at the small table.

I had warmed to Joss. She may have been some kind of cold vampire ninja, and maybe she was only doing her job, but I liked having her around. Partly because she'd saved my life, and partly because of her wicked cool hair. It made me wonder if there was a little party animal hidden under her strictly-business personality.

She hesitated a moment, then came and took a seat. She sat there, still as a statue as we ate, her face and expression covered by her cowl.

"Are there a lot of female Ebonguards?" I asked out of curiosity. It was honestly hard to tell.

Joss didn't reply, but Owen nodded. "Gender equality is one thing the vampire world has gotten right. Vampirism tends to even out physical strengths, and removing reproduction from the equation means there are less reasons to oppress or discriminate."

Lance leaned back in his chair. "Women also outnumber men as vampires. Maybe two to one. Women are much more likely to be turned, for one reason or another."

Realization hit me. "There were five women to two men on the Synedrion council. You'd never see that in the human world. Not yet."

"Four to three now," Owen grumbled.

"Oh, of course, Delphine is gone," I said. I tried not to vividly remember how she went. "A man replaced her?"

"Dante de Silva." Lance looked at Owen, and Owen looked back, their expressions concerned.

"That same creep who attacked Owen, jealous-lover style, when we first got here?"

"The very same."

"So we're screwed?" I put my spoon down. "He's not going to vote on our side, is he?"

Lance shrugged. "It was looking that way, until Owen came to beg for the Synedrion's aid in saving you. They had all but decided before then, but now they are debating again and still haven't made a decision. That might be a good thing."

"Really? Why?"

Owen shook his head. "I'm not sure. Maybe because the information we brought them meant taking down those who killed a member of the Synedrion, and it also meant recovering Kissare's chalice, an important relic long thought lost."

"A relic that can read the future? Although not necessarily accurately," I said. Despite the best efforts of the Starved and their leader, here I was, not pregnant. A small shiver ran through me, knowing that it didn't necessarily mean the prophecy wasn't true. Just that it hadn't happened *yet*.

"What's going to happen to the Starved that were caught?" I asked.

"The punishment for murdering another vampire is to be bound to the sun." Owen stabbed at his stew with his spoon, then left it alone, as though his appetite had gone. "There is a shrine on a low peak here in Umbravallis, where only a thin band of sunlight can enter. The Starved will be bound in there, and each day they will burn, inch by inch, not enough to kill them but enough to make them wish it did. Then each night they will heal, ready to repeat the process again."

"Yikes," I said. "That won't work for Scarl, though. He's human now."

"No." Owen looked down at his food, deciding to eat again. He mumbled through a mouthful, "It may be Alam's dagger for him."

"You vampires and your fancy terms. Alam's dagger, bound to the sun, Kissare's chalice ..."

"The dagger and chalice are some of our most sacred relics from the original seven." Lance leaned back in his chair and eyed Owen. "Along with other items, like Tiamat's Ring."

I looked at Owen too. "If we get through this, you're buying me a vampire history book so I can get caught up." Then I looked over at Joss, sitting deathly still. "If it's so bad to kill other vampires, how come the Ebonguard can?"

I wasn't sure she'd reply, but she spoke before anyone else could answer, "We are allowed only when given the order. Our mission was to retrieve you. Any who stood in our way could be killed. But whenever possible we were to capture and return them for punishment."

"Ebonguard are renowned for their adherence to orders," Lance said. "They are very strict about it all. Failure is a three-strikes-and-you're-out sort of system." Lance said this so nonchalantly, but Joss's dark eyes twitched when he did.

Softly, I asked, "Did what Delphine do to you, and how we were taken, count as a failure?"

"I'm on my second strike," was all she said, her voice blank.

"And what does *out* mean?"

No one answered me that time.

I watched Joss for a few silent moments. For how little she moved, she could have been nothing but stone covered in black silk. But I found myself worrying about her.

Lance pushed his chair back from the table and dipped a tiny bow. "I had better let you two get some rest. I'm sorry. I forget how much human bodies need it. I will see what I can do for your cause.

Keep up hope."

He left, and Joss shadowed him out the door without a word, locking it behind them.

Owen and I ate our food, each of us quiet. There was so much to think about, so much to ask, and so much to say that it overwhelmed my fragile state. I shut it all out and just sat. Just ate.

When my bowl was licked clean, I pushed it back with a huge and happy sigh.

Owen asked, "Better?"

I sighed. "If they're going to kill me, let them do it now. I'll die full and clean and happy." Although, I was still tired, thanks to the blood loss and sheer lack of sleep that had been the norm for too long. I was delirious with exhaustion. Maybe that was where the incongruous sensation of happiness came from.

Owen stood and came over to where I sat. He reached for me, and I placed my hands in his, feeling a slight tremble there. I didn't know if it was mine or his. He guided me toward the bed and pulled back the covers. I tried to give him a smile but it didn't quite want to form. There was still so much left to say, and I was too tired to say it.

The mattress was heavenly soft and comfortable. Every one of my aching muscles tingled in delight as I stretched out horizontally between the warm, silky sheets.

Owen slipped under the covers next to me. My

hands found his, and we curled together.

He tucked me into the hollow of his body, and that whistling emptiness inside me closed up like it had never been there at all.

21

KAITLYN

From the moment my head hit the pillow until I awoke who knew how much time later, I knew nothing but oblivion. I jolted awake, confused and unsure where I was from the fog of bad memories from the passed days. The room was dark, and all was quiet and still.

We are still in the Synedrion estate. They are deciding our fate. They could come for us at any moment. My eyes snapped wide open with terror.

A panic attack hit me, and my hands patted the bed, trying to find Owen beside me. I couldn't find him, and then … there, his warm, resting body. His smooth, firm muscles.

My arms wrapped around him with a primal urgency. I pressed my face to his, my forehead against his cheek. I clung to him with greedy fingers. I needed him, to be with him, here and always.

He stirred, slowly at first. Then his arms came around me, drawing my chest tight into his. His face turned, and warm lips met my forehead.

His hands stroked along my flesh, touching me and finding the spots where tension had gathered the hardest—the points below my shoulder blades, the flesh of my lower back, and the base of my skull. His fingers went deep into strained muscles, and the rigidity loosened and let go like the air I moaned out.

My eyes closed. Sensations met and melded in the red-tinted darkness behind my eyelids. My pulse quickened. His hands moved over my flesh, touching me in a way that made me want him wildly.

He kissed my forehead again, sending vibrations through my body like an electric shock. My back arched. I sought his lips like they were an antidote to poison. The kiss lengthened and deepened, rough, craving kisses, drenched in desire, full of the frenzy of life and the panic of death. He took hold of my top and pulled it over my head, and I did the same for him. The muscles of his chest rippled under my fingers.

His head lowered then, first to my breasts and then lower, his hands sliding off my pants.

Lying on my back, I clawed my fingers into the sheets as waves of pleasure built inside me, filling me from my toes, zinging up through my heart, and tingling across my scalp. I cried out with an overwhelming fierce desire to fill myself with Owen until I burst into pieces.

I pushed onto my elbows, reaching down to Owen and he responded, crawling back up my body, laying down kisses all the way.

We moved together with a sense of urgency that changed and shifted and grew ever more intense, that left me gasping. My nails bit deep into the skin of his back, desperate to bring him closer, even though we couldn't physically get closer than we were.

"I love you," he breathed into my ear. "You're my Strawberry, always and forever."

Heat, and pressure, and a delicious aching need for release, for Owen, for relief, for more, grew so strong I screamed, holding nothing back, as though weeks' worth of tension and terror and unrequited desire, love, and loss exploded through me.

My hands grasped for him, my whole body driven my maddening passion and desire to crush him into my being until we were one and could never be separated again. "I love you too. I love you so much."

Owen let out a roar of pleasure. My eyes closed as he collapsed on top of me, his breath coming in and out of his mouth in a fast rhythm that slowed and then normalized as mine did. Our heartbeats found a calmer pace together. We stayed locked in that tight embrace, two halves of a whole, unwilling

to let go, as sleep took hold of us again.

It felt like hours later, hours of blissful, restful slumber, when I awoke to the smell of coffee.

That smell awoke a different kind of desire in me. COFFEE.

It had been so long. I glanced at Owen in the half light, and decided to let him sleep some more. Emotionally, he'd been through almost as much as I had. And he was still learning how to cope with having emotions again. Even regular never-been-a-vampire-for-a-while humans weren't good at dealing with their emotions. Life was hard. Life being imprisoned, tortured, and with the one you loved held at the mercy of vampires was even harder.

I slipped out of bed and into a fluffy, white dressing gown.

Tiptoeing into the living area, I found a mouth-watering breakfast laid out for us. Tea, coffee, milk, and a choice of juices. A dozen different breads, pastries, cakes, croissants, and pancake options. Poached eggs, crispy bacon, sausages, and potatoes roasted in butter and rosemary. Sliced watermelon, guavas, and blueberries. It could have been room service from a fancy hotel, but a small folded note in the middle of the hot and cold beverages had "From Lance" scrawled across the front. I took a sip of orange juice, remembering how important vitamin C was in helping iron absorption, as I poured out a coffee and stirred in way more sugar than I really should.

My first sip of coffee was like inhaling liquid life.

I unfolded the note. It read, *No outcome yet. They are still not ready to vote. I remember good food as being one of the best ways to pass time. I'm not the chef Owen is, but I hope you both enjoy what I could scrounge up.*

I smiled, wondering where he got it all. Did he do a run to the nearest human town for some groceries? Or did some of the vampires here spoil their favorite human thralls? And were the chefs here humans or vampires, if they had any at all? Owen explained to me once that he'd learned to cook after he became a vampire. Mostly to learn more about the restaurant industry, since he owned a number of restaurants and bars, to be able to better communicate with his chefs. But he could never taste the food he made. It became an abstract sort of art form for him, creating foods and flavors scientifically, analytically, visually without ever knowing their flavor himself. It was one of the reasons he took such great pleasure in feeding me when he first held me captive. To see the food he made being savored.

I slathered a croissant in butter and filled it with blueberries and maple syrup. I had never done it before, but it felt like a good idea. And if that was the biggest risk I took today, it would be a good day.

I was enjoying my first mouthful when the door

opened. I stiffened, my breath held, wondering if this was the moment.

Ewan, the doctor, entered. He had promised he'd be back for more of my blood. In a doctorly way rather than a vampirely way.

I held up my coffee to him and took a sip, demonstrating myself hydrating.

He shook his head. "Coffee? Not coffee. Drink water."

I snorted. And drank more coffee anyway.

I let him take his blood without resistance. I didn't see the point. He popped and swapped vacuum sample tubes, filling three of them.

"What's happening to all of these?" I asked, pointing to the samples.

"Tests," he said.

Duh, I wanted to reply, but waited, and he continued without prompting.

"The first samples were inconclusive. Apart from that you're an incredibly rare blood type, Rh Null. Which is why we've been unable to give you any blood transfusions."

"And here I thought there were only As, Bs and Os." For someone who had been vampire food more than once, I was shocked at myself that I'd never known my own blood type before. I'd never really had the need, in normal human medical terms. I had never even heard of Rh Null type before.

Remortality

Ewan gave me the kind of look you might give an imbecile, clipped his bag closed, and left.

I finished my blueberry croissant and coffee, then snuck back through the bedroom and into the bathroom, carrying my luggage with me.

My eyes went to the massive tub. It could probably hold a dozen people. The outside was carved marble that made little steps up into the tub, and on each step were scented candles and pretty little vases filled with colorful bath salts and delicately carved soaps.

I wasn't allowed a bath yesterday, but I was clean now, and had waterproof dressings. This might be the last bath of my life, so to hell with Doctor Vampire's rules.

I got the water running and spent some time sniffing the different fragrance options, settling on one that smelled of a fresh spring day and green grass, with the lightest floral tones and something that reminded me of sunlight. I shucked off my robe, applied a few waterproof dressings to my worst wounds, and entered the tub with a happy sigh. I floated there for some time, enjoying the ebb and flow of the water and the scent rising from it. I could feel months' worth of tension melting away.

After the bath, I stood in front of the mirror, combing out my matted hair, black and dripping. I figured that vampires maybe could see their reflections, since all the bathrooms here had mirrors. I stared into my own

eyes, rimmed in dark shadows, and at my sickly pale skin. These weren't my most glamorous moments, but there was a defiance in my expression that felt more beautiful than make-up could ever manage. The rebelliousness of life. After a good breakfast, good bath, and great sex, I felt ready for anything.

I dug through my luggage, seeing what Owen had packed in there. No comfort clothes for me today. I was ready for war. I found a classy yet sexy rose red gown, and matched it to black pumps with a red heel, and my richest crimson lipstick. I twined my hair into an elegant rope braid down the side and wrapped the length into a French twist in the way a helpful hair-stylist on set had once shown me how to do.

I removed the bandages from my torn throat. It was ripped and bruised in blotchy yellow and maroon patches on both sides, from the base of my ears right down to my collarbones. I left it uncovered, so the Synedrion could see what had been done to me. I knew vampires didn't feel empathy, but it made me feel as though I were being rebellious, letting it all be visible. The ugliness of it stood in stark comparison to my beautiful dress.

Owen opened the door behind me. Wearing just his boxers, he came up and held me from behind, placing his chin on my shoulder, careful to avoid touching my neck.

"You look beautiful, Strawberry."

I smiled wryly at him in the mirror. "What I am is ready to hear what the damned Synedrion has decided. And ready to deal with whatever their decision is. If they won't give us their verdict soon, then I will burn this place to the ground, Owen. I will."

"I'll light the match myself," he replied.

We smiled at each other. Resolve hardened between us. We were done being pawns in this vampire game. We were done being held prisoner and waiting for vampires to decide if we should live or die.

It turned out we didn't have to wait much longer.

By the time Owen had dressed, choosing a suit and red shirt to match my gown, and we'd both eaten some more breakfast, there was a knock at the door.

The sound of a deep bell ringing in the distance followed it.

Our time was up.

Dread came in but so did courage. I was finished being jerked around by these vampires. Live or die, I wanted an answer, and I wanted it then.

Lance appeared. His face was grim. "They have finished debating. They are ready to vote on your fate."

22

KAITLYN

Every step I took reminded me that I was alive, and I wanted to stay that way. My muscles flexed and rolled. Long, determined strides carried me quickly to the council chambers, past the creepy statues, through the heavy, carved doors.

This time, the chamber was full. The Synedrion hadn't managed to keep me and my blood a secret, so obviously didn't see the point in keeping this meeting private as they had the last one.

No one made a sound as we entered. My eyes roamed across the crowded space and to the seven on their raised thrones. The sound of my breath and heartbeat seemed very loud in this quiet, lifeless place.

We were met at the door by Niamh who led us to the front of the dais.

Owen held my hand, and I kept my head up, leading with my chin. Refusing to look down or away, or to be cowed by what might be our sentence and fate. I was ready.

The thrall who gave the announcements seemed to be near the end of formalities, having started before we arrived.

Bertha gave me a smile, but she also licked her lips like she wanted to eat me. Lin and Shirina leaned toward each other, whispering enthusiastically. Dante's fingers gripped the armrests of his throne with blatant aggression. I wondered how he made the cut for joining the Synedrion. I honestly had no idea if this was some kind of monarchy or democracy, or something else entirely.

After the thrall had finished, Toren said, "We rule here today on a matter that concerns all vampire kind. With either outcome, there will be ramifications. Heavy ramifications. The Synedrion has deliberated on all concerns surrounding this issue and spent many hours debating."

Viatrix no longer seemed to be asleep. She looked down upon me, her head tilted and owl-like. She remained silent. Milton snarled and turned his face away, disgusted.

I began to sweat, my fingers shaking inside Owen's grasp. He squeezed them gently.

"We have spoken long on this issue, we have

made our decisions, and we are ready to vote," Toren said, standing to look down upon us with his dark, wrinkled eyes. "Those in favor of death for the humans."

Milton, Viatrix, and Dante raised their right hands high, as though summoning down lightning. I waited for more movement, my heart drumming like the thunder that should follow.

I couldn't breathe.

"Those in favor of allowing the humans to live."

Toren, Lin, and Shirina raised their hands. A moment after, Bertha followed.

Four to three. We were to live, four to three! Breath rushed back into me in shaky bursts.

I looked up at Owen, and saw hope and relief shining through his eyes, as I'm sure it did in my own.

A roar came from the crowd, a cacophony of applause, disbelief, and dissent. It was clear not everyone in attendance was thrilled that we weren't going to be murdered. Voices rang out.

"Give them Alam's dagger!"

"I want the cure!"

"Death to the vampire killers!"

I shrunk away, my relief short-lived. Regardless of the vote, of the verdict, the population was split, violently, in their opinion of us.

"Quiet!" roared Lin. The room settled. "We are not savages. Not animals. You must understand

this human is important to our whole society. Her blood could offer a method for those who wish to become human again to do so, and based on our recent research, may offer even more."

Dante grunted. "Forget the woman. Raine deserves punishment for his recent and past crimes."

I turned to look up at Owen, but caught Lance's gaze on the way. He stood still, frowning, watching from the side of the room.

"You could provide us with no proof of these alleged crimes, and the vote has been made," Toren said. "Being as they are humans who aren't held to vampire law, and that they acted in self-defense, there is to be no punishment for them for the vampires, the Starved, they killed."

A cry came from somewhere in the crowd. "Destroy them both! They will bring a plague of final death to us all!"

Milton turned his anger toward Shirina. "If you're going to keep your lab rat, you should keep her locked up as one. Humans are food or slaves. Letting her go free is a mistake."

A clamor of agreement rose from the crowd.

"If you don't give me my freedom, if you keep me as a slave, I will kill myself, and you'll have no blood for your tests," I threatened.

The crowd cheered, as though they liked that idea.

Shirina's eyes narrowed. "Then I would simply keep

you under thrall and have total control of your actions."

I narrowed my eyes in return. I wouldn't be beaten by these vampires. But I could play by their rules. "You don't have the right to keep me in thrall. I don't belong to you."

Owen's hand tensed in mine, and I squeezed it in return before letting it go. I hoped he understood what I was doing, that it was only for our freedom, and nothing more.

"I've been claimed by Lancelot Ferland, as has Owen. We are his, and he alone can choose what form our freedom now takes." The words were hard to say, but Owen had explained to me how seriously being claimed was in the vampire community. It would mean we were Lance's property, with very similar laws protecting that.

Lance seemed surprised by the announcement at first, but with a quick nod, he showed he understood. He came to stand by my side. "It's true, I have claimed them."

"Thank you," I whispered under my breath.

I wrapped my arms around his and hung on his side, dropping my gaze subserviently, as though I were his obedient and fawning property. I hated doing so, especially with Owen right beside me. How fake it felt compared to our real love. But I was an actor, after all.

I could feel the intensity of Owen's emotions. I

prayed that he wouldn't act on them. Being perceived as under Lance's ownership was a hell of a lot better than being a vampire scientist's thrall.

"It seems as though you have claimed her." Lin's eyelashes fluttered in a perturbed way. "So be it then. They will be your responsibility. You'll be expected to keep your property safe and under control."

"Of course," Lance said with a bow.

Grumbles rose from the crowd.

Toren boomed over them, "What this human can give us, through her blood, is of remarkable value. Not only for those who want to become human again, but all vampires. She and her companion, the vampire remade human, have our protection and the protection of the Ebonguard. That is the Synedrion's ruling."

That only made the rabble louder. Lin spoke up, "Beyond the ruling of us seven, Kissare's chalice shows her to live free."

That shut the room up. Apparently, this chalice was something to be taken seriously.

"And we have only regained the chalice, thanks, in part, to the humans," she followed up. Soft murmurs replaced the fanatical yelling.

She eyed Lance again next. "And of course, there are conditions to her freedom."

Still clinging meekly to Lance's side, my lower lip trembled but I bit it, defiantly, then spoke for myself. "Conditions?"

Shirina nodded. "We have already discovered much from your blood, but will require fresh samples for the foreseeable future to continue our work. You are to make these available to us as needed."

"Do we have to stay here, in Umbravallis?" I asked, my hope deflating.

"That will depend on your owner, human," Milton snarled.

Shirina waved his comment off. "We can have the samples collected anywhere and couriered as needed. We aren't relying on messenger pigeons," she said, with a tiny eye-roll. "Wherever you and your owner do go, however, you will always be watched by the Ebonguard. For your protection."

Bertha said, "Those are the terms we can live with."

We can live with.

We could live.

We would live!

And we would be free. Thanks to Lance, and my acting skills. And Owen for checking his jealousy. Maybe putting up the appearance of being claimed wasn't complete freedom, but it was a hell of a lot better than the alternative.

Elation made my heart sing, and my blood run hot through my veins. Tears filled my eyes. "Thank you."

Lin gave me a regal nod and clapped to the thrall who stood at hand, who announced the end of

proceedings and signaled for the crowd to leave the hall.

The crowd swirled, and heated conversation sprang up all around as the chamber cleared. I stood there, unable to move, as though my feet had grown roots like a tree and bound me to the ground.

Lance stepped out of my grasp. "Clever," he said.

Owen inhaled deeply, and his voice came out as a low growl. "As long as you don't take advantage of the situation."

"I'm sure he won't," I said. "And thank you for going along with it. I hope it won't mean too much trouble for you."

Lance smiled for a brief second only. "You? Trouble? Never."

We stood in our small triangle, silent for a moment.

Lance cleared his throat. "Don't worry about keeping up appearances of any kind regarding your relationship with Owen. Being with a human does not discount my claim over you, if I allow it. Only your obedience to me is important to display, in public, of course."

He patted Owen on the shoulder then, and left to speak to Niamh.

Owen put his arms around me, and we stood in a still embrace until the room was quiet again. When we split apart, I saw only Bertha, Lin, Lance, and our Ebonguard escorts remained in the chamber.

Bertha and Lin studied us with bright, interested eyes. I imagined Lin's was a scientific interest, but I wasn't sure about Bertha's.

"You know," Lin said, "beyond the rare blood type, we could find nothing remarkable about you or your blood … at first. We even sent agents to track and test others with Rh Null-type blood. We sent for blood samples from all those related to you by blood. There was not a thing we could find or replicate about your ability."

A painful fire lit inside me. "Did you … are they alive?"

Lin waved off my concern. "Our Ebonguard are very good, unlikely to be overcome by a desire for sweet blood. Not that any of the other candidates were found to be so desirable. We knew you were unique, but we didn't know why. Then, something very interesting happened.

"The blood sample that was taken after your return from the Starved has some significant changes. It now contains somatic cells that behave and replicate like pluripotent cells. It's incredible. Not only might we be able to create a cure for vampirism, but your blood might also hold the key to creating artificial human blood. The moment we found that, we called for the vote. That was all we needed to see to know we had to keep you alive."

"My blood … changed?" My voice cracked. Did it

change from the ceremony the Starved had held, their weird blood magic? Or something else afterwards? The lowest parts of my stomach churned. The Starved had wanted a cure for their thirst, a way that meant they didn't have to drink from humans, and they'd said my child would do that for them. But if Lin and her scientists could create an artificial blood, wouldn't that be fulfilling their prophecy, in a different way, without a child?

Lin was speaking again, but my thoughts blocked her out at first. I finally focused.

"… no special indicators, no passed-on traits. Owen is apparently purely human now."

Bertha tilted her head at that, blinking at us with her large eyes. "Owen saved you. You should know that."

I reached for his arm, clinging tight. "I do know that. If he hadn't brought help—"

"I don't mean bringing you back from the Starved," Bertha said. "Honestly, had we known where they were, we'd have sent for them sooner. They did kill a Synedrion member, after all. We just didn't know where they were. We've had no real reason to hunt them before. Despite their extremist fervor, their unwillingness to drink the blood of humans has generally been seen as unproblematic, no threat to other vampire activity. Owen did tell us where to find them, and that they possessed Kissare's chalice, but that's not how he saved you."

Bertha stood from her throne and walked down to us. Oddly, she seemed even smaller up close, fragile and sylph-like, forever caught in a gangly teenage growth spurt that made all her limbs seem too thin and long to support her modest height. "What I mean, is that Owen swayed my vote. When he came to plead for help, he told us how much he loved you. He begged to be turned again so he'd have the strength to fight for you. I wasn't sure before, when I first saw him. I thought maybe the change was only cosmetic. A surface thing, just a glamor of warmth and clockwork heart. But I saw then that the change was real, something deep and profound. You didn't just give him back his human form. You gave him back his humanity."

I looked from her intense gaze up to Owen, who stared back at her, his mouth parted but silent.

And it's his humanity that I love in return. But I didn't think a spoken declaration of love to Owen was a smart idea so soon after I'd announced I'd been claimed by Lance.

I looked for him again then, but he must have left the room.

"I still fear the very many things that may happen with you in the world. I fear our enemies using you. I fear that you will bear a child as the Starved saw visions of in the chalice, but I also fear that child and its powers may not be what they believed. The visions of the chalice are notoriously true yet open to mixed interpretation. I fear much, but what I fear most is war within our ranks."

Owen's hand came back to mine. "I can understand all those fears, and no matter what your reasons, I thank you for voting for us to live."

Bertha smiled. "How could I not? Your humanity was wonderful to see. That you could love in such a way, a way so many of us have forgotten even exists, made my decision easy. It also gave me hope. Reckless hope. And I have made the decision I will be one of the first to take the cure, when Lin and Shirina confirm it is safe."

I didn't know what to say. Owen bowed to her then, a sign of respect at her decision that seemed so right, I joined him.

Bertha smiled in a wistful sort of way, then turned from us. She met with Lin at the door, then both left without looking back.

Owen and I stood in the center of the huge chamber, alone except for the Ebonguard, who were to be permanent shadows in our lives. I could deal with that. It was a better outcome than I'd been imagining in my nightmares.

I looked at Owen, and swung my arms up around his neck, swaying as though slow dancing with him. "You saved me. You wanted to be a vampire to save me, but it was because you're not that we're alive. It was your being human that saved us both."

His eyes shone. His lips curved upward. "I think you're right."

I was, and he knew it.

"I want to go to the beach." Tears lay in my eyelashes. "As soon as we get back to the US, I want to go to Malibu and go to the beach. I want to swim and lie on the hot sand and … and forget. I want to forget all of this, Owen."

His hands reached around my waist, his fingers clasping at the small of my back. He rocked side to side with me, our cheeks together.

"Me too," he said. "There's so much I have to learn about being human again. I was scared I had only just begun and was about to meet my end." His forehead creased, eyebrows low over his pale blue eyes. "It's been so long since I felt really alive, Kaitlyn. I spent so much time just watching time pass. There was always so much of it, that it didn't seem to matter. Now I have … I don't know how much time I have, and somehow that makes it all so much more precious. I want to make each moment really count."

I let my tears of relief spill down, wetting both our cheeks. "I don't know how much time I have either, Owen. Death is the bill we get handed when we're born, and no human escapes having to pay

it, unless they become a vampire, I guess."

"I don't mind knowing I'm going to die. I'm happy knowing it, in fact. If I could live five hundred years without you or five minutes with you, I'd take those five minutes and squeeze every drop of living I could out of them and be content that it was enough. No, not enough, because I *could* live forever with you, but … but even five minutes is enough, in its own way. Does that make sense?"

I squeezed my eyes closed, but tears still poured freely. "It makes perfect sense."

It did. I felt exactly the same way. I had been willing to die, as long as I would die at his side, but I would equally be willing to live with him for all eternity.

I couldn't live without him.

He was my whole heart.

Time passed, but we stayed there in each other's arms, just being together and being alive. We had a future coming and we had no idea what it would bring, but we would explore it together until death took us.

23

OWEN

The lies I spoke stung my heart, and made my lips taste bitter.

They told me it was my humanity that had saved us, and it was my humanity Kaitlyn loved, but fear had crept into my soul. Fear, and a loathing of my weak, mortal form.

I hadn't saved Kaitlyn. Everyone else had. Joss, and Lance, and the Ebonguard, and the Synedrion, and Kaitlyn herself—they all saved Kaitlyn. I hadn't even been able get to her fast enough without being carried like a damn child.

I spoke of only desiring to spend every precious moment with her. I didn't know if I really believed that was enough. The idea of watching her die, whether now or of old age, filled me with a primal

fear that ate painfully at my insides. We had a future again now. We'd been given a reprieve, but the future terrified me. I was terrified I would fail Kaitlyn again.

I was failing her right now with my thoughts.

I couldn't win.

Part of me thought Kaitlyn knew how much I was struggling. She showed me how to do ten-minute meditations to help calm myself when my thoughts spiraled.

I found them useful when the Starved were delivered their punishments.

We were expected to be present at the trial of the Starved leader. He was quickly judged as guilty of Delphine's death, and being as he was human again, he was to take Alam's dagger, a sentence reserved for only the most wicked.

There was little mention of him being a Scarl. Some thought we'd been mistaken, that he couldn't be, that any physical indications were a trick of our minds. Either way, there was no proof left to speculate on. He was only human now.

He was held right in the middle of the council chamber, between two Ebonguard, as the dagger, a curved thing of jagged, black metal and a fire opal hilt, was brought out of its ceremonial case, and plunged into his heart.

Kaitlyn gasped beside me as his body and his

clothing transmuted into stone before our eyes, starting at the point the blade struck his heart, and travelling outwards. He screamed until his lungs were hard rock and he breathed no more. His head and limbs drooped, his death faster than the change, and he became an odd and disfigured statue.

Kaitlyn buried her face in my chest. "All the statues out there, is this what they are?"

I nodded, stroking the back of her head, as though my hands could wipe the memories and trauma from her mind. "I think this is only the second time it's been used on a human. Vampires don't die from it until they are completely stone. Some believe they don't die at all. But there's no way to know."

"That's terrible," Kaitlyn whispered.

"Not as terrible as what is to come next."

It was before dawn that the rest of the captured Starved were taken to the Sun Shrine for their punishment.

It wasn't often vampires were bound to the sun. We ... *they* generally respected the law not to kill each other. I'd only ever experienced one receiving such punishment before, so I knew what to expect.

Seeing, and hearing, what happened to that vampire that one time, was enough to make me know I never wanted it to happen to me. That was back when Adelle was still with me, and I with her, and I had been looking for any possible way of being free of her. I think she knew. She was the one to arrange being present at the sun binding ceremony. She wanted to make it clear I'd never be free. A vampire couldn't kill another vampire. Not without suffering a fate worse than death.

Even then, I was a man of resources, and I'd turned every one of them to finding a way to end her and the torment she'd caused me. I'd learned about the original seven, about their relics and the powers they were said to have. About a ring that would bring an untraceable death to those who received it.

The story I'd told Kaitlyn, and others, and myself, all those years wasn't the complete truth. Even if I began believing it myself. The ring didn't find its way to its victims on its own.

It was hidden now, in the safest place. It wasn't the kind of thing one could carry around on their person. But if anyone ever found out what I'd done with that ring, or even the fact that I had it, that I knew where one of the seven most sacred items in vampire culture was, then I'd be out there in the Sun Shrine myself. I had no doubt they would turn me again just so I could suffer that death.

Kaitlyn and I didn't have to be spectators to the Starveds' punishment, and we didn't want to be. But the location of the Sun Shrine, right near the entrance to the Synedrion's estate cavern, sat in a way that amplified the screams from those being punished throughout the valley.

Remortality

The anguished howls of the Starved reached us, even within the closed rooms of the Synedrion estate. We tried to sleep through it, but their cries were as relentless as the pain they suffered. It would take days, or weeks, for them to succumb, for their bodies to finally give in and be unable to heal themselves. Until then, all of Umbravallis would be in a state of mourning. Even vampires didn't have the stomach for this.

But Kaitlyn and I would be leaving before then.

We awoke the next evening, grim and pale, as the haunting cries of the Starved ceased, the night bringing them a reprieve before their torture began anew.

I slid out of bed and took several long breaths. Kaitlyn was already up, drinking coffee at the window and looking out at the artificially lit cavern that surrounded the palace.

She said, "They want to draw some of my blood today, and afterward, we will be allowed to leave, with Lance's permission, of course."

We were well and truly on vampire time. Even Kaitlyn spoke as though the days were nights and nights were days. But the silence from the Starved was all I needed to know the sun did not shine. I kissed her forehead. "Are you ready to go home?"

"Any version of yes I said would be an understatement." Her brow wrinkled. "It feels like we've

been here forever, but it hasn't really been that long at all. Maybe two weeks? I don't know. Time went funny so long ago." She shrugged. "Would you like some coffee?"

"I would. I'll get it, and I'll get you a refill on that one. Just let me get dressed first."

When I came back into the living room, still buttoning up my shirt, Lance was there. In Kaitlyn's hands was a book. Something small and bound in old leather with gold patterning. Had Lance given it to her?

"Thank you," she said. "About time I got caught up on some more vampire history."

I frowned. I didn't like that she needed, or wanted, to know vampire history, or that Lance had given her a book about it when she'd asked me for one. I still didn't like that for all intents and purposes, he now owned her, and me. At least under the eyes of vampire law. I still worried he would take advantage of that. All I could do was hope he wouldn't. But if he did, I knew exactly what to do to him.

"A little going-away present. I wanted to give you something, since you've given me, given *us* so much," he said. He looked down at his feet, then to the window. "I've also come to escort you to the lab. It's on the way to the airport."

"Can't Doctor Bedside Manner take the blood?" Kaitlyn asked.

"Lin and Shirina would like to see you again, so they prefer you come into the lab on your way."

Kaitlyn huffed. We were already packed, just waiting for the official word we were free to leave.

"Let's get out of here already," she said. She hopped up, and I admired the spring in her step. "Oh, one more thing."

She dashed off to the bathroom, and returned with a few bottles of bath salts and toiletries. She quickly unzipped her suitcase and stuffed them inside. "What?" she said, in response to my laugh. "A girl's got to get some perks from all this."

When we reached the car waiting for us in the driveway, two Ebonguard were there as well, loading heavy black duffle bags into the back. I'd been told one of our shadows was Joss, although Ash had apparently been assigned to some other task, so I didn't know our new second bodyguard.

Lance carried our suitcases for us with ease and loaded them in too. I noted that he wasn't using thralls anymore. He really had changed.

It was a short drive to the lab. Part of a large complex slightly away from the main town, it was a black, block-like building with smooth, clinical walls, and high-tech security. Floodlights lit the area all around, making it hard to see the stars in the night sky above.

In the foyer, Lance spoke through the intercom,

and the door opened for us automatically. We walked down the long white hallway, past rooms where scientists worked away at high-end sampling and analysis apparatuses. Lin and Shirina headed this research institute, but science was an area I'd never held an interest in, and what they did here was beyond me.

We reached a lab where Shirina sat looking into a huge microscope. Lin came in through a back door. They both wore white coats, protective glasses and gloves, and smiled to Kaitlyn, waving her over. Kaitlyn settled into a chair and chatted with Lin and Shirina, as though they were everyday human pathologists drawing her blood.

Lance and I waited at the door. I looked over at him as he continued to watch Kaitlyn, and her blood, with an intense expression. His gray hair always made him seem older and wiser than I had ever been, although he didn't have many more years on me. But he had been wiser, for a time. I'd looked to him for guidance for centuries.

"Will you take the cure, when it is ready?" I asked.

Lance raised an eyebrow. "It certainly has some temptations. But I don't think I will. I still hold a fear of mortality that is greater than my desire to see the sun again. I can protect Kaitlyn better if I stay this way too."

I watched his expression closely. He spoke of fear,

but he didn't seem to experience it in the raw, primal way in which I now did. He didn't experience any emotions in the way I, or any other human, did. Yet, he seemed to feel them more than a vampire would. "You have changed, though, since you tasted her. You sound more like the vampire you once were. The vampire who was my mentor. Do you still have the feelings her blood brought to you? Or has it all faded?"

He frowned. "Mostly faded now. That sensation of empathy, real empathy, where I hurt to even see the pain I'd caused the two of you, it's all gone. But it acted as a reminder to me. Of what it was to be human, of why I'd chosen to follow a moral path even as a vampire."

"You'd forgotten, at one stage," I said.

"I did. Something happened, and, I guess the anger I felt for humankind made it hard to remember why I'd ever cared about them. Maybe that's the true curse of being a vampire—not having a sense of guilt or understanding of the frailty and preciousness of human life."

We both watched as Shirina finished taking her blood samples, and checked on Kaitlyn's other injuries, making sure they were clean and healing properly.

Lin held Kaitlyn's hand, then spoke something quietly into her ear. I couldn't hear it. I wondered if Lance did.

Lance stiffened slightly. He sighed and said, "I

never told you that I had a family."

I frowned, unsure exactly what he meant. Vampires couldn't procreate.

"Before I was a vampire," he clarified. "I'd had children, before I was turned. And those children had children. I had two beautiful great-granddaughters of my own blood, even when I knew you. In a way, that's what kept me on a moral path for so long, and what knocked me right off that path."

"I never knew," I admitted.

"I kept it secret. My secret joy. Until one night, a man whose life I had spared, who I'd drunk from and set free, as was our way, went on to attack my descendants. He did terrible things to them. And so I did terrible things to him. I took the revenge that they couldn't. But that revenge had a cost. What happened to him was blamed on them. Because of my actions, my great-granddaughters were burnt as witches. They burned under the midday sun, and I watched from the shadows, unable to go into the light to save them. After that, I could no longer find any reason to spare human lives."

I didn't know what to say. I'd known something had happened, something that had changed him within the space of a week from a logical and moral man to a violent animal. Something that had destroyed him and our friendship.

Kaitlyn arrived back with us, looking both pale

and flushed.

Lance nodded to her. "Until now," he said. "Thank you again, dear Kaitlyn, for making me the man I once was."

"I'd say no problem, but, well ..." She gestured to everything around us, as though it summed up the trauma of the past two weeks.

"Maybe one day I'll be able to make it up to you." He reached for her hand and placed a kiss there.

I inhaled sharply, jealousy spiking unbidden. I tried to fight it away. He was my friend. *Our* friend. "Is everything fine? What did Lin have to say?"

"Huh?" Kaitlyn seemed distracted. "Yes, fine. Nothing. Let's get out of this place, okay?"

"Yes," I said. "Let's go home."

24

KAITLYN

We were driven to the airport, the same one we'd once arrived at by helicopter. It felt like so long ago. A small private jet awaited us there, the windows blacked out for the Ebonguard who were escorting us.

I stepped out of the car without a single backward glance at the dark valley of vampires. I was done with it, and I never wanted to see the place again, not even in my dreams, although I was sure it would haunt me.

My spirits were flying at full mast. Home. We were going home. Back to Los Angeles. Sunny and warm days, lemony yellow sunlight. Palm trees and ocean breezes, and wide boulevards with houses that were shiny new. Movie stars, and swimming pools, and life.

Owen said his goodbyes to Lance as I stared up at the spatter of stars in the sky high above, breathing my freedom in deep.

Lance leaned in to kiss my cheek goodbye. Owen turned and stalked away, up the steps of the small jet. As our perceived owner, he explained he didn't always have to be near us. He would say he'd sent us away without him on some errand. Claimed humans were often used by vampires for tasks in the human world. And he would come to visit us often, to maintain the illusion of his claim on us. The Synedrion didn't seem to really care, as long as the Ebonguard escort was always with us.

Lance gave me a small smile. "Look after yourself. I know you think you love him, but be wary of a relationship built around so much trauma. It makes it hard to see how little you really know each other."

I took a deep breath. I did love Owen, with all of my soul, but Lance's words echoed the exact same fears and worries I'd had myself, before I had so much more to fear. There was a lot I didn't know. But finding out was what would come next. Owen and me, living together, getting to know each other, loving each other, being alive together. Growing our relationship and our love. And I was looking forward to it.

"See you soon, Lance."

His black eyes glistened under silver eyebrows.

"Just look after yourself. Until we meet again."

I left without another word.

I met Owen at the top of the stairs, and we turned our back on the world of night behind us. The Ebonguard were somewhere on the plane, but they made themselves scarce, giving us our privacy.

I almost laughed in surprise when a human attendant, the same who'd flown with us to Owen's castle originally, came out with a smile. What were the odds? "Hello again, you two. This is my first time to this airport. Did you have a good getaway?"

Owen burst into laughter. I managed to stop giggling long enough to say, "I think we're making a perfect getaway now."

"We'll be off in a few moments," she said. Still smiling, she nodded and headed back behind the curtain.

Owen and I took our seats. Our luggage was there, and our phones were too. I grabbed at mine, the reality of life beyond the estate and the dungeon settling into me in a way it hadn't until then. That feeling of connectedness, of normality that came as I turned the phone on, couldn't be overestimated. My eyes swept across the screen to see hundreds of missed calls, emails, and text messages.

Many were from my agent, and I opened an email then gasped, my hand going out to clutch at Owen's sleeve.

"What is it?"

"My agent's been trying to reach me. I have a new part waiting for me when we get back. The one I really wanted." My eyes went wide, reading over the details. It was on another big-budget film, a supporting part, but a big one. A good one. The actress they had for the role had to bow out, and filming started very soon.

Owen wrapped an arm around me as the plane headed toward the sky. "I'm proud of you, Strawberry, and I love you."

"I love you too," I said. My voice was small and distracted.

The plane lifted higher, then smoothed out and we winged our way west, out of Europe and toward home.

My stomach rolled. I tried to breathe through the wave of anxiety that hit me. Back at the lab, Lin had confirmed my suspicions. There was a reason my blood had been different since returning from the Starved.

I wasn't becoming a vampire, as I'd worried at first. Shirina had confirmed that. Luckily, I hadn't lost enough of my own blood for the Starved blood that had made it into my system to take hold. It was something else, that had happened since then.

I didn't know what my future held. I didn't know if I could take the new movie role. I didn't know if I could continue to be an actress at all, or a normal human in any respect. The one life dream that had given me so much determination in the past now felt out of reach again in a way it never had before. After everything that had happened, and could happen, and would happen next, could I still follow those dreams?

Maybe I should, in spite of it all.

At least for as long as I could before my life changed forever.

The plane hummed and sang. I hit the screen fast and sent a brief message to accept the part before I changed my mind.

A wave of dizziness swamped me.

Owen watched me closely. He ran a finger down my clammy cheek. "Strawberry, are you all right?"

My eyes filled with tears.

My lips, numb and stiff, barely moved. "I'm pregnant."

Kaitlyn and Owen have more to lose than ever, but they are safe now, right? RIGHT?

FIND OUT IN

ABOUT THE AUTHOR

Lena Fox is a pen name of Selina Fenech. Professional daydreamer, Selina Fenech writes "adorably dark" Epic and Urban Fantasy for teens and adults. Filled with sweet and quirky characters, laugh out loud moments, and breath-taking adventures, her unique worlds are perfect for readers who love thrilling twists paired with happily ever afters.

Artist, mother, and cancer survivor, Selina is determined to live life to the fullest, and loves escape rooms, gardening, and all forms of food and geekery.

Selina also applies her distinctive take on magical realms as a world-renown fantasy artist and has published many illustrated books, oracle decks, and colouring books.

FIND OUT MORE
ABOUT SELINA

Official Website www.selinafenech.com

NEED MORE TO READ?

Discover more urban fantasy, paranormal romance, contemporary romance, young adult, epic fantasy, fairy tale retellings and more from Lena Fox and Selina Fenech.

Visit www.selinafenech.com
to sign up for a free sampler library!